GOING TO GUIDES

HEY KIDS COLOR ME IN!

GOING TO
MAGIC KINGDOM
A GUIDE FOR KIDS & KIDS AT ♥

by Shannon W. Laskey

THIS BOOK BELONGS TO A SUPER-COOL PERSON NAMED:

_____

Orchard Hill Press

This book is dedicated to the memory of brothers Walt & Roy Disney

A Note From the Author

Back when I lived in Los Angeles, an airline messed up my flight and, to make it up to me, they gave me a free round-trip ticket to anywhere they flew in the United States. Can you guess what I said to that? "I'M GOING TO WALT DISNEY WORLD!" My friend Elizabeth was living in Florida at the time and had just recently quit her job at the resort. Her ex co-workers were nice enough to give us free tickets for Magic Kingdom, Epcot, Disney's Hollywood Studios—then called Disney-MGM Studios—and Pleasure Island, which has since been turned into part of Disney Springs. It was my first time visiting Walt Disney World and, of course, it was fabulous. I remember it was so odd to walk into Magic Kingdom and feel like I was in Disneyland, knowing I was nowhere near it!

Fast-forward many years to the launch of my Going To Guides series with *Going To Disneyland: A Guide For Kids & Kids at Heart* and later *Going To Disney California Adventure: A Guide For Kids & Kids at Heart.* The number one question people asked me was, "Are you going to create a book for Florida?" My answer, of course: YES!!! I was SO excited to go back and visit Walt Disney World again on "Research Expeditions."

Most people love their "home park" best and Disneyland will always be the most special to me but I love, love, LOVE Magic Kingdom. I hope this book makes your visit there even more wondrous than it would have been and helps you to notice, understand and appreciate the magic of this extraordinary place.

If you're an adult reader with no kids in sight, I warmly welcome you. I created this book series for kids **AND** kids at heart like you—and *me!* Thanks for joining in the fun.

xoxo,
Shannon

Jumping for JOY in Magic Kingdom!

ABOUT THE AUTHOR

Shannon W. Laskey thought of the idea for Going To Guides when she went to her local library to get a kids' guide to Disneyland for her older son and found out there weren't any. Going To Guides are written, designed and illustrated by Shannon with additional art and photos by contributors. Shannon lives near San Francisco with her husband—who's like Kristoff, oldest son Ed—who's like Peter Pan, and youngest son Clark—who's like Jiminy Cricket. As for Shannon, she's like the Cheshire Cat since she tells people which way to go.

©2017 Shannon W. Laskey. All rights reserved.

Edited, Proofread, Fact Checked and Fine-Tooth Combed by Hugh Allison

Front cover and spine illustrations and photographs by Shannon W. Laskey
Front cover castle photograph by Dave DeCaro
Back cover illustration by Kirsten Ulve

LEGAL MUMBO JUMBO	WHAT IT MEANS
No part of this publication may be reproduced, distributed or transmitted in any form or by any means, including photocopying, recording or other electronic or mechanical methods, without the prior written consent of the author, except in the case of brief quotations in critical reviews and certain other non-commercial uses permitted by copyright law.	Don't copy this book, okay?
This book is neither authorized nor sponsored nor endorsed by The Walt Disney Company or its subsidiaries. It is an unofficial and unauthorized book, and not a product of The Walt Disney Company.	This book is NOT made by Disney!
All products, services and mentions of names and places associated with The Walt Disney Company, its businesses and other companies independent of The Walt Disney Company are not intended to infringe on any existing copyrights or registered trademarks of their respective companies, but are used in context for educational purposes.	The stuff talked about in this book is owned by other people. We're just telling you about it.
The opinions and statements expressed in the quotations and text are the opinions of those people who are quoted and do not necessarily reflect the opinions and policies of The Walt Disney Company and its subsidiaries nor the author or the publisher.	The quotes in this book are what the person who said it thought and might not be what Disney, the author or the publisher thinks.
While every precaution has been taken in the preparation of this book, no responsibility is taken by the author or the publisher for errors or omissions. Neither is any liability assumed for damages resulting, or alleged to result, directly or indirectly from the use of the information contained herein.	We tried not to make any mistakes while writing this book but if we did, well, these things happen. (But if we did, we're sorry!) (And if you notice something that's a mistake, will you let us know?)

Printed in the United States of America
ISBN #978-09995721-0-8
Orchard Hill Press

For more information on Orchard Hill Press, visit www.OrchardHillPress.com
For more information on Going To Guides, visit www.GoingToGuides.com

Magic Kingdom Details

Lovely Liberty Square gazebo

A wagon loaded with supplies in Frontierland

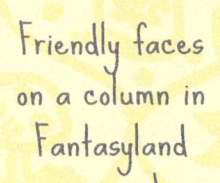

Friendly faces on a column in Fantasyland

Cool plantlife in Tomorrowland

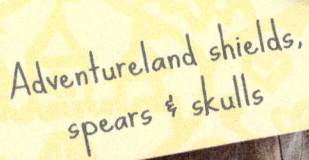

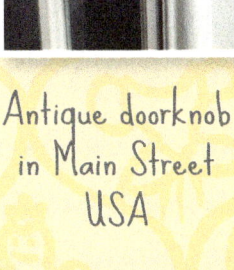

Adventureland shields, spears & skulls

Antique doorknob in Main Street USA

"Second star to the right and straight on til morning!"
—PETER PAN

Table of Contents

SECTION	PAGE
Disney Dictionary	8
Special Stuff in This Book	9
My Trip Planner	11
Itinerary	12
Packing List	13
About My Plans	14
Countdown	15
Walt Disney's World	17
Visiting Magic Kingdom	27
Main Street USA	49
Fantasyland	65
Tomorrowland	99
Liberty Square	119
Adventureland	133
Frontierland	151
The Rest of the World	167
My Trip Journal	181
About My Visit	182
Scrapbook	184
Autographs	186
Heartfelt Thanks	189
Contributor Credits	190
Game Answers	191
Index	192
The Pixie Dust Game	194

What's the game plan? → Itinerary

How did Magic Kingdom come to be? → Walt Disney's World

The park's 6 themed lands → Main Street USA ... Frontierland

What's the rest of Walt Disney World like? → The Rest of the World

Create a scrapbook about your visit! → Scrapbook

Collect character autographs here → Autographs

Disney Dictionary

Here are some Disney words and phrases to know before you go:

A **ATTRACTION**—Things at the park to see, do or ride are called attractions. These can be anything from a treehouse to a live show to a roller coaster.

AUDIO-ANIMATRONIC—Magic Kingdom has Audio-Animatronic figures in many attractions. These are a type of robot that moves and makes sounds but stays fixed in one spot.

C **CAST MEMBER**—In a play or movie, the performers are called the cast. The people who work in Magic Kingdom are performing their jobs for the park's visitors, so they are called Cast Members.

D **DISNEY LEGEND**—People who have made an extraordinary contribution to The Walt Disney Company are named Disney Legends—a sort of Hall of Fame for Disney employees.

G **GUEST**—Magic Kingdom calls its visitors Guests and loves to make them feel special. If you ever have to sign for something in the park, Cast Members will often ask for your autograph instead of your signature.

H **HIDDEN MICKEY**—The shape of Mickey Mouse is hidden in attractions, shops, restaurants and other places around the park. These Hidden Mickeys are sometimes made to look like Mickey's whole body but usually are the simple three-circle symbol that looks like his head. You'll also find Hidden Mickeys on toys, clothing, mugs and other goodies.

I **IMAGINEER**—This term is a combination of the words "imagination" and "engineer." It describes the talented people who create the magic in Disney parks. They design and oversee every detail, from the machinery that will make a ride work right down to the pattern of the wallpaper inside a restaurant.

R **RIDER SWITCH**—Some, but not all, rides offer this option. One Guest stays with a non-rider while the rest of their group enjoys the ride. Then the Guest that stayed behind uses a Rider Switch pass to ride alone or with one other person without having to wait in line.

Special Stuff in This Book

Look out for these handy-dandy symbols and features!

HOT TIP

The **Hot Tip** symbol is found near insider info that not just everyone knows about.

SPY

Eye Spy symbols let you know about special things to spy with your little eye.

If you love to color, you may enjoy coloring in the **black-and-white images** in this book. Sharp colored pencils or colored ballpoint pens will work best.

HEY KIDS COLOR ME IN!

SO YOU KNOW... blah, blah, blah

These **So You Know** areas explain a little bit more about words or phrases you might not know, like "memento mori," "topiaries" and "croon."

Indoor Boat Ride · est. 1971 · Calm & Mellow

This **stamp** tells you what type of attraction it is, what year it opened in Magic Kingdom and what it's like. Slower attractions are "Calm & Mellow," faster attractions are "Wild & Thrilling" and the ones that are somewhere in between are "Lively & Exciting."

There's a **scrapbook** on pages 184 and 185. While you're in Magic Kingdom, save any tags, receipts, tickets and other flat things so you can add them to the scrapbook later.

The fun doesn't have to stop because you're standing in line. Play **Waiting Games** when you're waiting for a ride, sitting in a restaurant or just taking a break. Time flies when you're having fun.

FUN FACT

The smiley **Fun Fact** symbol is found near extra tidbits of fun and fascinating trivia.

MAY BE SCARY

If you see this **caution sign** in this book near info on an attraction it means that some people find it scary. If you're unsure, ask a Cast Member working at the entrance to that attraction what to expect.

★ ★ ★ ★ ★ ★ ★ ★ **WORDS TO THE WISE** ★ ★ ★ ★ ★ ★ ★ ★

There are lots of activities, games and fill-in-the-blank areas in this book. A ballpoint pen or pencil will work best. Don't use markers because the ink might bleed through to the other side of the page. Also, the maps in this book are not to scale and have been simplified to not show every single path or feature.

The Roger E. Broggie train pulls into Main Street station to take Guests around the park on the Walt Disney World Railroad.

My Trip Planner

Use this handy Trip Planner to get ready for your visit to Magic Kingdom!

My Trip Planner—Itinerary

How excited are you about visiting Magic Kingdom? Draw an arrow from the black circle below to the word that best describes how you feel:

SO YOU KNOW... itinerary = detailed plan for a trip

excited-o-meter

FAIRLY PRETTY VERY BEYOND

Date(s) of your visit to Magic Kingdom: ....

How many days will you be there? ....

Who are you going with? ....
....

Will you be going anywhere else in Walt Disney World? ☐ Yes ☐ No

If yes, where? ....
....
....
....

Will you be staying in a hotel? ☐ Yes ☐ No

If yes, what's it called? ....

My Trip Planner—Packing List

What are you going to bring with you?

My Trip Planner—about My Plans

*NOTE: Fill this page out **after** you've read this book.*

Which **ATTRACTIONS** do you want to do?

....

....

....

Which **CHARACTERS** do want to see?

....

....

....

Which **ENTERTAINMENT** do you want to see?

....

....

....

Which **FOOD & DRINKS** do you want to try?

....

....

....

My Trip Planner—Countdown

How many days until you go to Magic Kingdom? . . . .

When it's exactly 10 days before your visit, start this countdown by coloring in the 10 circle. Each day, fill in the next shape in the countdown until it's time for your trip. For days 10–2 use a black crayon or colored pencil. For the last day, color in the bowtie with red to complete the picture.

Wahoo!
You're going to Magic Kingdom!

GOING TO
MAGIC KINGDOM
✦ OFFICIAL FAN CLUB MEMBER ✦

This Card Hereby Certifies That:

_____

is a Fan of Going To Magic Kingdom

This Member is a: ☐ Princess ☐ Prince ☐ Villain

☐ Other _____

Member Since: _____

Going To Guides
PO Box 217
Lafayette, CA 94549
www.GoingToGuides.com

Going To Guides APPROVED BY Laskey Going To WDW

GOING TO
WALT DISNEY WORLD
✦ OFFICIAL FAN CLUB MEMBER ✦

This Card Hereby Certifies That:

_____

is a Fan of Going To Walt Disney World

This Member is a: ☐ Princess ☐ Prince ☐ Villain

☐ Other _____

Member Since: _____

Going To Guides
PO Box 217
Lafayette, CA 94549
www.GoingToGuides.com

Going To Guides APPROVED BY Laskey Going To WDW

Would YOU like to be in the Fan Club?

Fill out the cards above and—POOF!—you're in the club.
If you'd like to get actual cards or other fun goodies
like bookmarks, buttons, gift tags and stickers
—all made from art in the Going To Guides books—
visit the "GoingToGuides" shop on Etsy:
www.etsy.com/shop/goingtoguides
If you share pix of you with your goodies or book
on Instagram, Facebook or Twitter, be sure to
tag @GoingToGuides so we can see too!

GOING TO GUIDES

Walt Disney's World

What Will You Find in This Chapter?

THE MAN BEHIND THE MOUSE
It all started with a man

HATS OFF TO CHARACTERS!
Can you match the hats to their owners?

MAKING DISNEY MAGIC
What came afer Mickey?

WEST COAST VS. EAST COAST
How are Disneyland Resort and Walt Disney World Resort different?

THE HAPPIEST PLACE ON EARTH
Before Magic Kingdom there was Disneyland

FUN AT THE WORLD'S FAIR
Disney and the 1964 New York World's Fair

THE FLORIDA PROJECT
Walt dreamed of a new world in Florida

BROTHERLY LOVE
Brothers Walt and Roy Disney were quite a team

COWBOYS DON'T BELONG IN SPACE
About Magic Kingdom's utilidors

A MAGICAL KINGDOM
Everything got off to a great start

WHAT ELSE WAS POPULAR IN THE 1970s?
A look at trends when Magic Kingdom opened

R.I.P.
Some attractions that are goners

A Whole New World

The #1 Most Visited Theme Park in the #1 Most Visited Vacation Resort is Magic Kingdom in Walt Disney World! Millions of people travel to Florida from all over the globe each year to enjoy this extraordinary place. Walt Disney World is made up of four theme parks—Magic Kingdom, Epcot, Disney's Hollywood Studios and Disney's Animal Kingdom—plus water parks called Typhoon Lagoon and Blizzard Beach. There's also lots and lots of hotels, a shopping and dining area called Disney Springs, golf courses, a campground and more. Whew! This wonderland covers a whopping 43 square miles—which is about the size of the city of San Francisco. So, why is it called Walt Disney World? It's named after the fellow who started it all.

★ The Man Behind the Mouse

Walt Disney said his company began with a mouse but without Walt, there would have never been a Mickey. Growing up in the Midwest in the early 1900s, Walt loved to draw and was a cartoonist for his school paper. His career began in Kansas City, Missouri where he worked at an art studio, an advertising agency and his own animation studio before moving to sunny California to start a new animation studio with his big brother Roy. Their first big success was a short black-and-white cartoon called "Steamboat Willie" starring the one and only Mickey Mouse.

TIME MACHINE

1901 — Parents Elias & Flora welcome Walter Elias to the Disney family on Dec. 5th in Chicago, Illinois—the fourth of five children.

1923 — The Disney Brothers Cartoon Studio makes its debut & is later renamed the Walt Disney Studios.

1928 — "Steamboat Willie," starring Mickey & Minnie Mouse, hits theaters.

1937 — Disney's first full-length animated movie "Snow White & the Seven Dwarfs" hits theaters.

Hats off to Characters!

From **Mickey** to **Moana**, there are now **thousands** of Disney characters. Draw a **line** connecting the character's **name** with their **headgear**. The first one's been done for you. *Answers on page 191.*

Mickey Mouse
Steamboat Willie, 1928

Dopey
Snow White and the Seven Dwarfs, 1938

Pinocchio
Pinocchio, 1940

The Mad Hatter
Alice in Wonderland, 1951

Nana
Peter Pan, 1953

Mary Poppins
Mary Poppins, 1964

Prince John
Robin Hood, 1973

Jafar
Aladdin, 1992

Kuzco
The Emperor's New Groove, 2000

Russell
Up, 2009

Dr. Facilier
The Princess and the Frog, 2009

Fix-It Felix
Wreck-It Ralph, 2012

Judy Hopps
Zootopia, 2016

Moana
Moana, 2016

1950
The greatest adventure of them all! Disney's first full-length live-action movie "Treasure Island" hits theaters.

1955
The first Disney theme park—Disneyland!—opens in Anaheim, California about 30 miles south of Los Angeles.

1964
The Walt Disney Company debuts new attractions at the New York World's Fair that later make their way into Disney parks.

1971
Five years after Walt Disney's death, Walt Disney World opens in Orlando, Florida.

> "Once there was a princess."
> —SNOW WHITE

★ Making Disney Magic

After creating many more black-and-white cartoons, the Walt Disney Studios released their first *color* cartoon in 1932, *Flowers and Trees,* which earned them the first of *many* Academy Awards. Soon after, Disney's *Snow White and the Seven Dwarfs* took the world by storm—the first full-length **animated** movie. Over the next several years, the Walt Disney Studios created *animated classics* like *Pinocchio, Fantasia* and *Dumbo.* In 1948, the studio began a nature *documentary* series called *True-Life Adventures* and later got into the **live-action** business with movies like *The Story of Robin Hood and His Merrie Men, 20,000 Leagues Under the Sea* and *Westward Ho, the Wagons!* The popularity of *television* swept the nation in the 1950s and replaced radio as the main way people were entertained at home. While most movie makers looked at *TV* as competition, Walt and his team began creating television programs that let people know about their movies and projects. The first show began in *1954* and was called *Disneyland.* It was all about how a brand-new theme park was being built in California.

FUN FACT
The soundtrack for "Snow White & the Seven Dwarfs" was released in 1938— the first time a movie soundtrack had ever been sold to the public.

SWEET!

SO YOU KNOW...
animated = cartoons
live-action = real people

West Coast vs. East Coast

DISNEYLAND RESORT	WALT DISNEY WORLD RESORT
Located in Anaheim, California	Located in Orlando, Florida
About 500 acres in size	About 27,000 acres in size
2 theme parks	4 theme parks
50+ rides	45+ rides
0 water parks	2 water parks
0 golf courses	Several golf courses
3 Disney hotels + 1 on the way	18+ Disney hotels + 1 on the way
Downtown Disney shopping area	Disney Springs shopping area

★ The Happiest Place on Earth

As Walt's career grew, so did his *family*. He and his wife Lillian had two daughters, Diane and Sharon. The legend goes that one day as Walt was sitting on a bench watching his daughters enjoy the *merry-go-round* in L.A.'s Griffith Park, he dreamed of a clean, beautiful theme park where all the visitors were treated like first-class guests. Walt's dream came true when *Disneyland* opened on July 17th, 1955. After a rocky start, the park became a gigantic success. Though Disneyland had *plenty* of visitors, not as many came from the eastern part of America so Walt had a new idea—to create a *magical kingdom* on the East Coast.

DISNEYLAND, 1958

Fun at the WORLD'S FAIR

Way back in the mid-1800s, **enormous expos** that showcased the latest ideas and inventions from different nations began to take place. People traveled from **all over the globe** to be dazzled by special exhibits and attractions created especially for these fairs. In 1964-1965, America hosted the **New York World's Fair** where The Walt Disney Company debuted four brand-new attractions.

AT THE FAIR	AFTER THE FAIR
Carousel of Progress	After a run in Disneyland (1967-1973), this attraction moved to Magic Kingdom.
It's a Small World	Versions of this ride can be found in Disneyland, Magic Kingdom, Tokyo Disneyland, Disneyland Paris and Hong Kong Disneyland.
Great Moments with Mr. Lincoln	An Abraham Lincoln Audio-Animatronic appears in Disneyland and Magic Kingdom's The Hall of Presidents.
Magic Skyway	Technology from this attraction was used to create PeopleMovers in Disneyland (1967-1995) and Magic Kingdom.

★ The Florida Project

> **SO YOU KNOW...**
> **prototype** = original model that other versions copy

Walt had **big plans!** He wanted to create something bigger, better and different from Disneyland in California. A lot of other businesses had crowded in on Disneyland so the **#1 goal** was to get plenty of land—which he found in Florida! Walt's original vision was to create a theme park like Disneyland with a nearby airport, business center and brand-new type of planned city called the Experimental **Prototype** Community of Tomorrow. This *futuristic city* was going to be an always-changing place where new technologies would be tested including:

- A giant climate-controlled dome
- A no-cars-allowed downtown
- Multiple levels of underground roads
- PeopleMover & monorail electric transportation

Sadly, in the middle of planning all of this, Walt Disney passed away. Missing their *dynamic* leader, The Walt Disney Company focused on creating Magic Kingdom. This new park was designed to have a layout like Disneyland with a train station at the entrance and an old-fashioned Main Street ending at a fairytale *castle*. The main difference with the *Florida Project* was that there was lots more space to work with!

Brotherly Love

The *Sharing the Magic* statue by Blaine Gibson in Magic Kingdom's Town Square pays tribute to **Roy Oliver Disney**. Walt and Roy Disney were quite a team. Walt would dream up the creative **ideas** and Roy would make sure they could **afford** them! It was Roy who **first** moved to Los Angeles, where he worked as a banker. After Walt moved out West too, the pair started their own company and went on to work together **all their lives**. After Walt died, Roy set aside his plans to retire to make sure **Disney World** would still be created without Walt. Roy said the new resort needed to be called **Walt** Disney World as a tribute to his brother so that people would **always remember** the man behind the magic.

> "We're going to finish the Florida park, and we're going to do it just the way Walt wanted it."
> —ROY DISNEY

Cowboys Don't Belong in Space

One day, Walt Disney was in Disneyland and didn't like the sight of an employee dressed as a **cowboy** walking around futuristic Tomorrowland. To solve this issue for Magic Kingdom, a system of tunnels for **employees only** were built so that Cast Members could move through the park without being seen by Guests. These **"utilidors"** were constructed as a first floor and covered with dirt dug up when making **Seven Seas Lagoon**. Cast Members can **avoid crowds in the park** and move quickly through the utilidors on foot, by bicycle and in battery-operated carts. This **underground complex** is home to the park's computer systems, tubes for moving trash, and a wardrobe department as well as employee-only cafeterias, lockers and a hair salon.

SPY: The entrance to Magic Kingdom is **level** with Seven Seas Lagoon but, as you walk towards Cinderella Castle, notice how the ground gradually goes **uphill** to make room for the utilidors underneath.

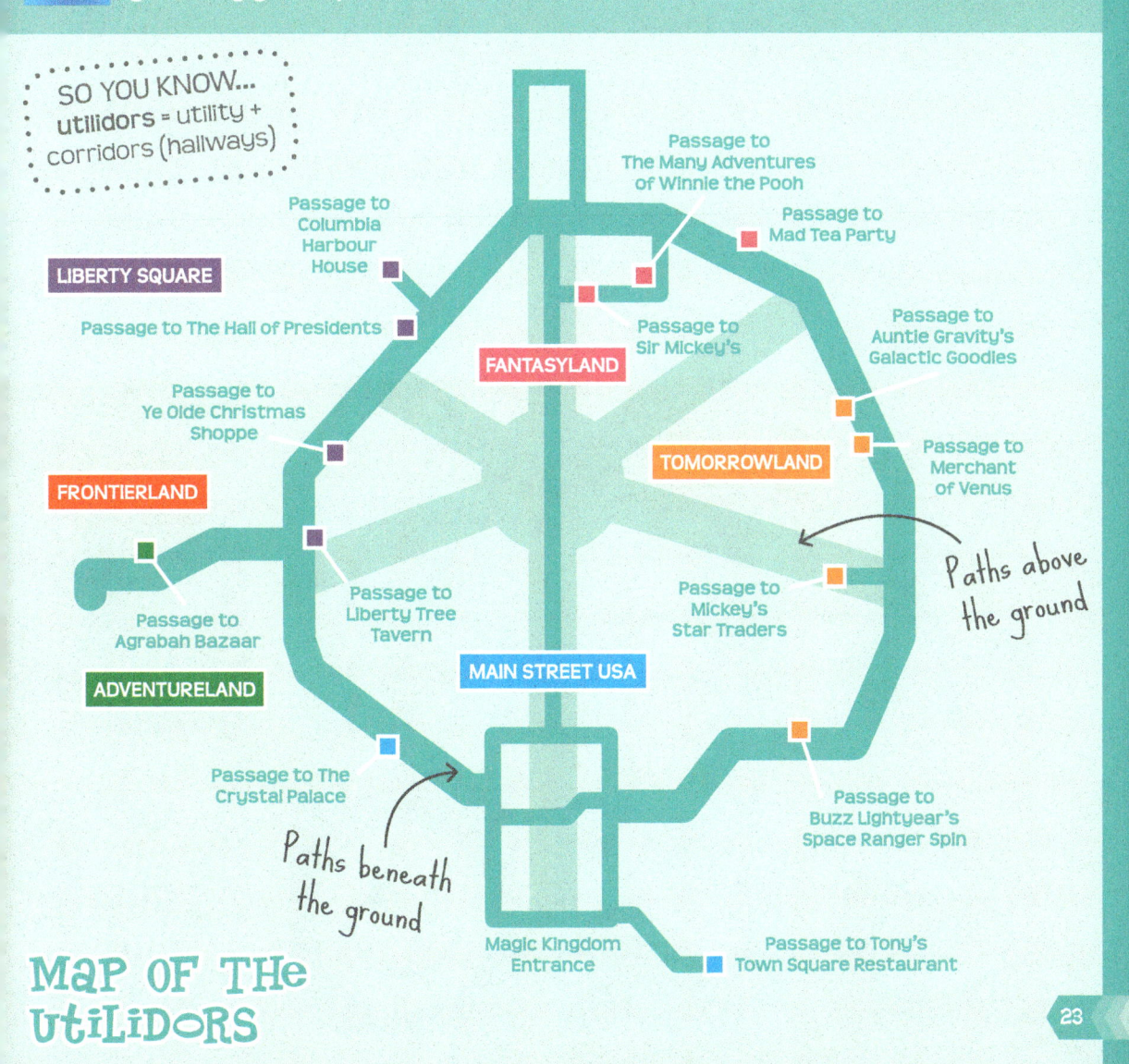

Map of the Utilidors

SO YOU KNOW...
utilidors = utility + corridors (hallways)

- Passage to Columbia Harbour House
- LIBERTY SQUARE
- Passage to The Hall of Presidents
- Passage to The Many Adventures of Winnie the Pooh
- Passage to Mad Tea Party
- Passage to Sir Mickey's
- FANTASYLAND
- Passage to Auntie Gravity's Galactic Goodies
- Passage to Ye Olde Christmas Shoppe
- TOMORROWLAND
- Passage to Merchant of Venus
- FRONTIERLAND
- Passage to Mickey's Star Traders — *Paths above the ground*
- Passage to Liberty Tree Tavern
- Passage to Agrabah Bazaar
- ADVENTURELAND
- MAIN STREET USA
- Passage to The Crystal Palace — *Paths beneath the ground*
- Passage to Buzz Lightyear's Space Ranger Spin
- Magic Kingdom Entrance
- Passage to Tony's Town Square Restaurant

Magic Kingdom, Opening Day, 1971

FUN FACT

Roy Disney stood with his brother's best friend Mickey Mouse to deliver a dedication speech at the Grand Opening Ceremony. Today, you can find his words on a plaque near the flagpole in Magic Kingdom's Town Square.

COOL!

★ A Magical Kingdom

Walt Disney World opened on Friday, October 1st, 1971 with *Magic Kingdom* and the Contemporary and Polynesian Village hotels all connected by the *Walt Disney World Monorail* just as they are today. About 10,000 people paid around *$5* for park admission with ride tickets. At the *Grand Opening Ceremony* later in the month, Guests enjoyed a grand *parade* with marching bands and characters, and a choir singing *When You Wish Upon a Star* as thousands of balloons filled the sky. The new park was an instant success!

What Else Was Popular in the 1970s?

- Disco
- Feathered Hair 
- Mood Rings 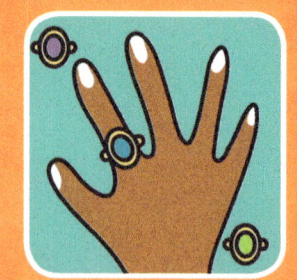
- Pet Rocks 
- Platform Shoes 
- Roller Skating 
- Smiley Faces 
- Wild Wallpaper

R.I.P.
SOME ATTRACTIONS THAT ARE GONERS

1971–1999
Skyway
Guests were treated to a bird's-eye view of the park in suspended gondolas that carried them between Fantasyland and Tomorrowland.

1971–1998
Mr. Toad's Wild Ride
Guests rode in out-of-control motorcars through Mr. Toad's hair-raising adventures—now the site of The Many Adventures of Winnie the Pooh.

1971–2012
Snow White's Adventures
Mine carts carried Guests on this dark ride through Snow White's sometimes scary story—now the site of Princess Fairytale Hall.

1971–2001
Mike Fink Keel Boats
Flat boats like the ones Davy Crockett and Mike Fink raced in carried Guests around the Rivers of America.

1973–1983
Plaza Swan Boats
Lovely swan-shaped boats ferried Guests back and forth past Cinderella Castle and Swiss Family Treehouse.

1971–1994
Davy Crockett's Explorer Canoes
Cast Members in coonskin caps helped Guests paddle around the Rivers of America.

1971–1994
20,000 Leagues Under the Sea: Submarine Voyage
Guests enjoyed a submarine ride past interesting underwater sights like mermaids and sea serpents—now the site of Seven Dwarfs Mine Train.

25

Everywhere you look in Magic Kingdom, you'll find lovely flowers and plants.

Visiting Magic Kingdom

What Will You Find in This Chapter?

MAGIC KINGDOM'S LANDS
See what the six themed lands are all about

KNOW BEFORE YOU GO
Make the most of your Disney experience

JUST SOME OF THE SEASONAL FUN
Events that only happen at certain times of the year

THE MAGIC OF MAGICBANDS
What are these special wristbands for?

ADD TO THE FUN WITH FASTPASS+
The ins and outs of FastPass+

AT A GLANCE CHARTS
Attractions, Entertainment, Food & Drinks, Meet n' Greets and Shops

NO ONE LIKES A LINE
Special features make waiting more fun

RAZZLE-DAZZLE
About fireworks and parades

TOP 4 PLACES TO BEAT THE HEAT
Where to cool off on a hot day

TOP 5 YUMMY SNACKS
The best bites

CONTAIN YOUR EXCITEMENT
Souvenir containers make snacking special

WHERE'S MICKEY
Where to look for Hidden Mickeys

A VERY PRESSING MATTER
About pressed coins

SAY "CHEESE!"
Info on PhotoPass

TOP 6 SHOPS
Shops worth going in whether you're shopping or not

TOP 4 REST SPOTS
The best places for a break

CREATIVE OUTLETS
Where to recharge gizmos

TANGLED CHARACTER QUIZ!
Test your *Tangled* knowledge

KEY
- HELPFUL SPOTS
- PARADE ROUTE
- RESTROOMS

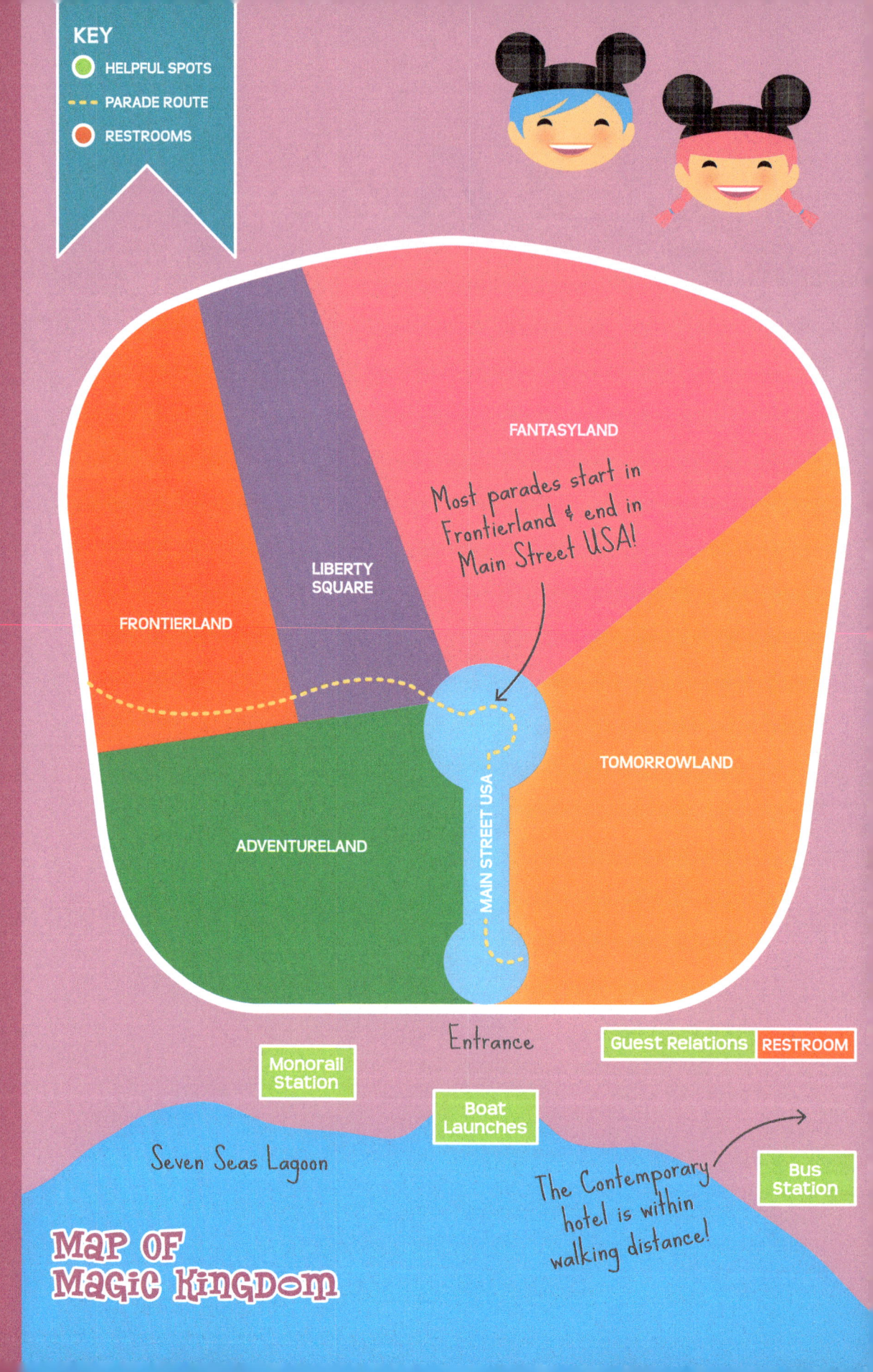

FANTASYLAND

Most parades start in Frontierland & end in Main Street USA!

LIBERTY SQUARE

FRONTIERLAND

TOMORROWLAND

ADVENTURELAND

MAIN STREET USA

Entrance

Monorail Station

Boat Launches

Guest Relations | RESTROOM

Seven Seas Lagoon

The Contemporary hotel is within walking distance!

Bus Station

Map of Magic Kingdom

"Have you ever seen anything so wonderful in your entire life?"
—ARIEL

A Most Magical Place

You're going to Magic Kingdom? *Fabulous!* With lots of classic *Disney charm* and the most rides of any of Walt Disney World's theme parks, pretty much every resort Guest has this park on their *bucket list.* Since there is so much to see and do, people who come from out of town usually stay for *several* days. Magic Kingdom—and Walt Disney World's three other theme parks—are open every day of the year, *even* Thanksgiving and Christmas!

HOT TIP Looking to avoid **crowds?** Attendance is highest during summer, the holiday season and special events like **marathons.** Some planning pros suggest avoiding Magic Kingdom on **Mondays** since many people arrive on Sunday and **start off their vacation** there the next day.

★ 6 Themed Lands

Magic Kingdom has different sections called *lands* and each has its own *theme* and unique look. If you've *already* been to Magic Kingdom, put a ✓ by your fave! If you've *never ever* been there, put a ✓ by the land you *think* you'll like best when you get there—then turn the page to see what the lands are all about!

- ☐ Adventureland
- ☐ Frontierland
- ☐ Main Street USA
- ☐ Fantasyland
- ☐ Liberty Square
- ☐ Tomorrowland

29

Magic Kingdom's Lands

Main Street USA
Stroll through a turn-of-the-century small town. Catch a lift in a vintage vehicle, hop aboard a steam train and find the perfect spot to watch a fabulous parade.

Fantasyland
Step into your favorite story. Coast through a glittering mine, dive into a mermaid's world and bounce in a honey pot with a beloved bear.

Tomorrowland
Discover the wonders of tomorrow today. Spiral through space, zoom in a zippy car and battle a robot army.

LIBERTY SQUARE
America's history comes to life. Get to know past Presidents, steam across waterways and brave a haunted house.

ADVENTURELAND
Exotic adventures await in this lush, tropical setting. Fly on a magic carpet, sail pirate-infested waters and sing like the birdies sing.

FRONTIERLAND
Mosey back to the days of the Wild West. Catch a bear-y delightful show, splash down into a briar patch and explore an untamed island.

31

What do you want to do most when you're in Magic Kingdom?
- ☐ Ride rides
- ☐ See live shows
- ☐ Watch parades
- ☐ Meet Disney characters
- ☐ Other

_____

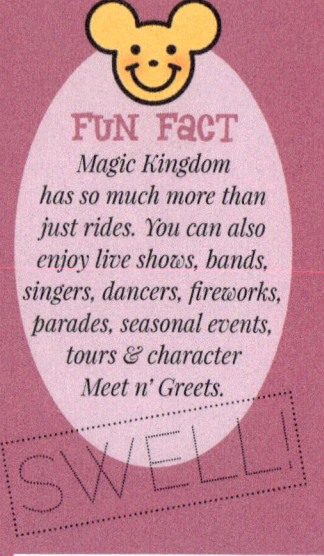

FUN FACT
Magic Kingdom has so much more than just rides. You can also enjoy live shows, bands, singers, dancers, fireworks, parades, seasonal events, tours & character Meet n' Greets.

SWELL!

★ Know Before You Go

So, what's the first step? Whoever is in charge of planning your trip will want to create a *My Disney Experience* account on the Walt Disney World website or the free smartphone *app*. With this account, you can plan and arrange everything for your visit. The app version lists your scheduled reservations for you like the web version but also has *up-to-the-minute* news on wait times, closures, and character locations. Handy, printed *maps* and *Times Guides* in the parks have info on parade routes, entertainment, minimum height restrictions and more. If you ever get confused, lost, or have a question once you're in Walt Disney World, ask any Cast Member for help!

HOT TIP If you're using the **My Disney Experience** app, take a **screenshot** of your plans so you can see them quickly without going back in the **app**.

Just Some of the Seasonal Fun

WINTER
- Holiday firework shows and parades
- Jungle Cruise becomes Jingle Cruise
- Meet Santa Claus
- Mickey's Very Merry Christmas Party *(costs extra)*

SPRING
- Easter procession featuring the Azalea Trail Maids
- Meet Mr. and Mrs. Easter Bunny

SUMMER
- Patriotic fireworks celebrating Independence Day

FALL
- Mickey's Not-So-Scary Halloween Party *(costs extra)*

PLUS
- Special themed food and drinks to celebrate various holidays and events year round

The Magic of MagicBands

Magical bracelets called **MagicBands** can be linked to your **My Disney Experience** account and used as your hotel **room key** and **park ticket**. You can also use them to check in to **FastPass+ lines**, link your **PhotoPass** pictures *(see page 43)* and pay for food, drinks and souvenirs. **How do they work?** The center of the waterproof wristbands have an **oval Mickey Mouse icon** that you tap to any of the hundreds of **touchpoints** all over Walt Disney World. MagicBands come in a variety of solid colors but you can buy fancy **character** styles, **charms** and other decorative **doodads**. There are also **MagicKeepers** which hold the icon in a **clip** instead.

HOT TIP You can link **more than one** MagicBand to your **My Disney Experience** account.

SPY See if your MagicBand unlocks **special surprises** on Haunted Mansion, It's a Small World, Space Mountain and **other places** around the resort.

Add to the Fun With FastPass+

BEFORE YOU ARRIVE
FastPass+ is a system where you can use a **special entrance** to skip the regular standby line at some attractions. You can make **up to 3** FastPass+ reservations for each day of your visit **up to 30 days** before your trip—or **up to 60 days** if you'll be staying at a Disney hotel—but all 3 reservations must be in the same park. Once you have a **My Disney Experience** account and a **park ticket,** you can start reserving FastPass+ experiences. One person in your group can create a **Family and Friends** list on their account to set up everyone's schedule together.

AT THE PARK
Your reservations won't be for an exact time—you'll have a **one-hour window.** Head to the location where you have your reservation anytime during that hour and use your **park ticket** or **MagicBand** to enter the FastPass+ area. Once you've used all your FastPasses, you can search for more (one at a time) using the **FastPass+ kiosks** dotted around the park or the **My Disney Experience** app. If you didn't make any reservations **in advance,** you can see what's still available when you're there.

HOT TIP **FastPasses** for popular attractions are snatched up quickly. If you can't get a reservation, you can try the regular standby line. Head to that attraction **when the park opens** for your best shot at a shorter wait.

33

Attractions at a Glance

KEY
- ✚ = FastPass+ available
- ❄ = Indoor experience
- ✿ = Rider Switch available
- ▲ = Minimum height requirement

MAIN STREET USA
- Main Street Vehicles
- Walt Disney World Railroad

FANTASYLAND
- Dumbo the Flying Elephant ✚
- Enchanted Tales with Belle ✚ ❄
- It's a Small World ✚ ❄
- Mad Tea Party ✚
- Mickey's PhilharMagic ✚ ❄
- Peter Pan's Flight ✚ ❄
- Prince Charming Regal Carrousel
- Seven Dwarfs Mine Train ✚ ✿ ▲38"+
- The Barnstormer ✚ ✿ ▲35"+
- The Many Adventures of Winnie the Pooh ✚ ❄
- Under the Sea ~ Journey of The Little Mermaid ✚ ❄
- Walt Disney World Railroad

TOMORROWLAND
- Astro Orbiter
- Buzz Lightyear's Space Ranger Spin ✚ ❄
- Carousel of Progress ❄
- Monsters, Inc. Laugh Floor ✚ ❄
- PeopleMover
- Space Mountain ✚ ❄ ✿ ▲44"+
- Tomorrowland Speedway ✚ ✿ ▲32"+ (passenger) ▲54"+ (driver)

LIBERTY SQUARE
- Haunted Mansion ✚ ❄
- Liberty Square Riverboat ❄
- The Hall of Presidents ❄

ADVENTURELAND
- Enchanted Tiki Room ❄
- Jungle Cruise ✚
- Pirates of the Caribbean ✚ ❄
- Swiss Family Treehouse
- The Magic Carpets of Aladdin ✚

FRONTIERLAND
- Big Thunder Mountain Railroad ✚ ✿ ▲40"+
- Country Bear Jamboree ❄
- Splash Mountain ✚ ✿ ▲40"+
- Tom Sawyer Island
- Walt Disney World Railroad

no one likes a line

If you ask a hundred people what they love most about going to theme parks, not one of them will say, **"Standing in line!"** To make the wait more enjoyable, **Imagineers** have created fun and **interactive** features to check out before it's **your turn** to ride these attractions:

Dumbo the Flying Elephant
- Frolic in a circus play area with rope climbs, trampolines and slides until a pager goes off letting you know it's time for your flight with Dumbo

Peter Pan's Flight
- Enjoy Tinker Bell's antics
- Get sprinkled with pixie dust
- Play with shadows

Seven Dwarfs Mine Train
- Play with musical fountains
- Sort different shaped gems
- Spin gem-filled barrels to make characters appear

The Many Adventures of Winnie the Pooh
- Bang on fruit and veggie drums
- Draw on a Hunny Wall
- Knock on a door to hear Piglet
- Play peek-a-boo with a gopher
- Spin sunflowers

Under the Sea ~ Journey of The Little Mermaid
- Sort objects with friendly blue crabs
- Visit with Scuttle the Seagull

Space Mountain
- Play video games

Haunted Mansion
- Be a muse to a dead poet
- Figure out whodunit from clues on five statues
- Play music on a creepy crypt
- Solve a puzzle on a haunted bookcase using this code:

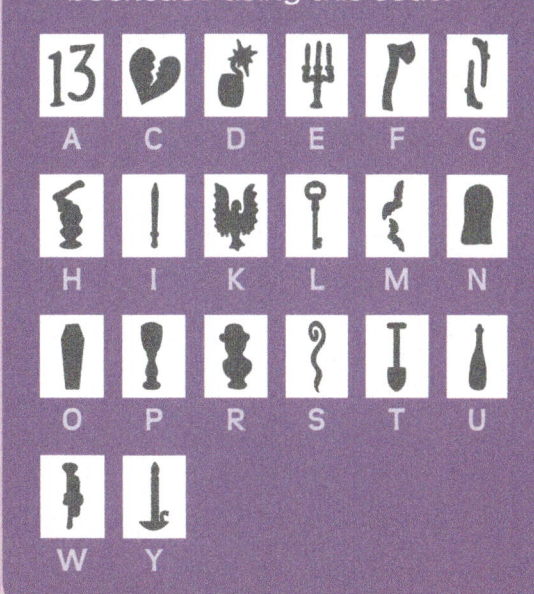

13	♥	🍍	♆	🪓	👂
A	C	D	E	F	G

👢	🗡	🦅	🗝	🦴	🪦
H	I	K	L	M	N

⚱	🏆	👤	❔	🔨	👔
O	P	R	S	T	U

👤	🗡
W	Y

Big Thunder Mountain Railroad
- Peek into the mine
- Set off detonators
- Test the air with an AutoCanary

HOT TIP: If you use **FastPass+**, you'll miss some—or **all**—of the cool features in the **regular standby line**. Also, if there isn't a long wait for an attraction, some parts of the line may be **closed off** to Guests.

entertainment at a glance

MAIN STREET USA
- Casey's Corner Pianist
- Citizens of Main Street
- Flag Retreat
- Let the Magic Begin
- Main Street Trolley Show
- Mickey's Royal Friendship Faire
- The Dapper Dans

FANTASYLAND
- The Royal Majesty Makers

TOMORROWLAND
- Dance Parties

LIBERTY SQUARE
- The Muppets Present Great Moments in American History

ADVENTURELAND
- Captain Jack Sparrow's Pirate Tutorial

MULTIPLE LANDS
- Firework Shows
- Main Street Philharmonic
- Parades

➡ Entertainment offerings and times often change so be sure to check current info

➡ The Times Guide doesn't list all entertainment offerings—if you have questions, head to City Hall, check the My Disney Experience app or ask a friendly Cast Member

➡ Frontierland is on the parade route but has no regularly scheduled entertainment—though sometimes there are surprise flashmob-style Hoedown Happenings

Razzle-Dazzle

Magic Kingdom delights Guests with lively **parades** and thrilling **firework shows** featuring **projection mapping**—a special effect where moving images are shown on buildings. Parades have included Festival of Fantasy, Main Street Electrical Parade and Mickey's Once Upon a Christmastime Parade. Firework shows have included Happily Ever After, Wishes and Celebrate the Magic. Be sure to check out the **schedule** during your visit!

HOT TIP Though you can see the fireworks from **many** locations—even outside the park—get a spot in **front of Cinderella Castle** if you want to see the **images** that are projected onto the castle as part of the show.

★ Top 4 Places to Beat the Heat

"I don't know why but I've always loved the idea of summer and sun and all things hot."
—OLAF

Feeling the heat? Cool down in these refreshing areas!

#1 Casey Jr. Splash Pad

There's water, water everywhere at the Casey Jr. Splash 'N' Soak Station in Storybook Circus. Happy camels, giraffes, elephants and monkeys from the circus train from *Dumbo* spray gentle jets of water while cute Casey Jr. shoots a cool, refreshing mist into the sky.

LOCATION: Fantasyland

SPY: Take a look at the **numbers** on Casey Jr.'s train cars! **71** is the year Magic Kingdom opened and **82, 89** and **98** are the years the other Walt Disney World theme parks opened.

#2 Cool Scanner

Right next to the Cool Ship snack stand is this outer space-themed water mister with a red spaceship on top.

LOCATION: Tomorrowland

#3 Leaky Tikis

Visit this row of carved tiki totems near Enchanted Tiki Room and they'll say Aloha with surprising sprays and spritzes of water.

LOCATION: Adventureland

#4 Splash Mountain

There's a reason the signs for this ride say You May Get Wet. As your log winds along the waterways, water often splashes into the boat but the big plunge near the end of the ride is where you'll really feel it!

LOCATION: Frontierland

Food & Drinks at a Glance

KEY
- 🟥 = Extra seating upstairs
- 🟢 = Indoor restroom
- ❄️ = Indoor seating
- 🔆 = Outdoor seating
- 🔶 = Open for breakfast

FULL SERVICE	QUICK SERVICE	ON THE GO
Sit-down meal with waiters	*Order then take to a table*	*Limited or no seating*

MAIN STREET USA
- **Full Service:**
  - The Crystal Palace 🟢❄️🔶
  - The Plaza Restaurant ❄️
  - Tony's Town Square Restaurant 🟢❄️
- **Quick Service:**
  - Casey's Corner ❄️🔆
  - Plaza Ice Cream Parlor ❄️🔆
- **On the Go:**
  - Main Street Bakery 🔶

FANTASYLAND
- **Full Service:**
  - Be Our Guest 🟢❄️🔶
  - Cinderella's Royal Table ❄️🔶
- **Quick Service:**
  - Cheshire Café 🔆🔶
  - Gaston's Tavern ❄️🔆
  - Pinocchio Village Haus 🟥❄️🔆
- **On the Go:**
  - Prince Eric's Village Market
  - Storybook Treats 🔆
  - The Friar's Nook 🔆

TOMORROWLAND
- **Quick Service:**
  - Auntie Gravity's Galactic Goodies 🔆
  - Cosmic Ray's Starlight Café 🟢❄️🔆
  - The Lunching Pad 🔆
  - Tomorrowland Terrace
- **On the Go:**
  - Cool Ship 🔆
  - Joffrey's Revive 🔆🔶

LIBERTY SQUARE
- **Full Service:**
  - Liberty Tree Tavern 🟥❄️
  - The Diamond Horseshoe 🟥❄️
- **Quick Service:**
  - Columbia Harbour House 🟥🔆❄️
- **On the Go:**
  - Liberty Square Market 🔆
  - Sleepy Hollow 🔆🔶

ADVENTURELAND
- **Full Service:**
  - Skipper Canteen 🟢❄️
- **Quick Service:**
  - Tortuga Tavern 🟥🔆🔆
- **On the Go:**
  - Aloha Isle 🔆
  - Sunshine Tree Terrace 🔆

FRONTIERLAND
- **Quick Service:**
  - Pecos Bill Tall Tale Inn and Café 🟢❄️🔆
- **On the Go:**
  - Golden Oak Outpost
  - Westward Ho 🔶

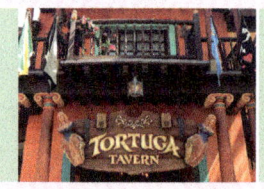

⇨ There are also snack carts and food stands
⇨ Full-service restaurants request or **require** reservations to be made in advance
⇨ Most quick-service and on-the-go places will give you free water in a to-go cup
⇨ Many Guests don't care for the taste of the resort's tap water and buy bottled water
⇨ Most restaurants have kids' menus and usually grownups may order from them
⇨ Vegetarian, vegan, kosher, allergy-friendly and nutritious options are available
⇨ Some restaurants have free coloring sheets for kids—and kids at heart

★ Top 5 Yummy Snacks

"Well I suppose there's time for dessert."
—YZMA

Which of these scrumptious delights sounds best to you?

#1 Dole Whip
This frozen soft-serve treat made with pineapple juice is actually dairy free! Enjoy your whip on its own or in a cup of pineapple juice as a float.
LOCATION: Aloha Isle

#2 Citrus Swirl
Similar to the Dole Whip, this sweet treat combines vanilla soft serve with frozen orange juice—YUM!
LOCATION: Sunshine Tree Terrace

#3 Mickey Ice Cream Bar
There are lots of Mickey-shaped goodies but this one may be the most delicious of all! Creamy vanilla ice cream is shaped like the main mouse and coated in chocolate.
LOCATIONS: Various ice cream carts

#4 Popcorn
Warm, salty popcorn fresh from the popper just tastes better when you're popping it into your mouth as you stroll around Magic Kingdom!
LOCATIONS: Various popcorn carts

#5 Churro
This sweet, crunchy treat is made from dough that's pulled through a star-shaped mold, deep fried and sprinkled with cinnamon and sugar. Olé!
LOCATIONS: Various churro carts

Contain Your Excitement
Why buy popcorn in a paper box when you can have it served up in **Cinderella's carriage**, a **Mickey balloon** or the **Seven Dwarfs mine car?!** Disney parks offer a variety of **specially shaped containers** for drinks, popcorn and other food. These fun choices are usually only around for a **limited time** and some are **so popular** that the parks have trouble keeping them in stock! The fanciful containers **cost extra** but you get to take them home as a **souvenir**.

> SO YOU KNOW...
> **souvenir** = something bought as a reminder of a place you visited

Where's Mickey?

There are **oodles** of **Hidden Mickeys** in Magic Kingdom. Put a ✓ in the box next to the ones you see.

MAIN STREET USA:
- ☐ On a Steinmouse & Sons piano in a window of the Emporium
- ☐ Upside down on a sign for lollipops in Main Street Confectionery

FANTASYLAND:
- ☐ In the rocks on the base of a statue in front of Gaston's Tavern
- ☐ In the shape of the rocks at the exit of Under the Sea ~ Journey of The Little Mermaid (when seen from just the right spot, it looks like Mickey in his *Steamboat Willie* outfit)

TOMORROWLAND:
- ☐ On a hair salon customer's belt buckle in one of PeopleMover's indoor scenes.
- ☐ On the front of a train on the mural inside Mickey's Star Traders.

LIBERTY SQUARE:
- ☐ On a framed chart inside Columbia Harbour House
- ☐ On George Washington's sword in a painting inside The Hall of Presidents

ADVENTURELAND:
- ☐ On a silver medallion embedded in the ground in front of Agrabah Bazaar
- ☐ On the sign for Jungle Cruise

FRONTIERLAND:
- ☐ A rope on the wall of Frontier Trading Post
- ☐ Gears on the ground at Big Thunder Mountain Railroad

My List

Here's where I found some more Hidden Mickeys:

_____
_____
_____
_____
_____
_____
_____
_____
_____
_____
_____
_____

Look near this to locate this!

KEY
◆ = Character dining
✚ = FastPass+ available
❄ = Indoor experience

Meet n' Greets at a Glance

MAIN STREET USA
- Classic characters
- Mickey Mouse ✚ ❄
- Tinker Bell ✚ ❄
- *Winnie the Pooh* characters ◆ ❄

FANTASYLAND
- *Alice in Wonderland* characters
- Ariel ✚ ❄
- Cinderella ✚ ❄
- Cinderella and other princesses ◆ ❄
- *Cinderella* characters
- Daisy Duck ❄
- Donald Duck ❄
- Elena of Avalor ✚ ❄
- Gaston
- Goofy ❄
- Merida
- Minnie Mouse ❄
- Peter Pan
- Rapunzel ✚ ❄
- The Beast ◆ ❄
- Tiana ✚ ❄
- *Winnie the Pooh* characters

TOMORROWLAND
- Buzz Lightyear
- Stitch ❄

LIBERTY SQUARE
- *Mary Poppins* characters
- *The Princess and the Frog* characters ◆

ADVENTURELAND
- *Aladdin* characters

FRONTIERLAND
- Country Bears

➡ Which characters you can meet, when and where changes—so check Character info on the My Disney Experience app or ask a Cast Member to be sure you don't miss any
➡ When meeting characters you can get a photo taken with them and ask for their autograph
➡ Some characters sign their name with a pen, some use a special stamp and others hand out pre-signed cards
➡ Many characters write VERY large so, if you want to try to fit a lot of signatures on one page, be sure to let them know before they start signing
➡ If you see a character walking quickly, they are probably headed for a break and won't have time to stop and visit with you

Shops at a Glance

MAIN STREET USA

- Box Office Gifts
- Crystal Arts
- Curtain Call Collectibles
- Disney Clothiers
- Emporium
- Harmony Barber Shop
- Main Street Confectionery
- Main Street Fashion and Apparel
- Main Street USA Silhouette Cart
- Newsstand
- The Art of Disney
- The Chapeau
- Uptown Jewelers

FANTASYLAND

- Bibbidi Bobbidi Boutique
- Big Top Souvenirs
- Bonjour Village Gifts
- Casey Jr. RailRoad Mercantile
- Castle Couture
- Fantasy Faire
- Hundred Acre Goods
- Sir Mickey's

TOMORROWLAND

- Buzz's Lightyear's Space Ranger Spin Photos
- Merchant of Venus
- Mickey's Star Traders
- Tomorrowland Light & Power Co.

LIBERTY SQUARE

- Liberty Square Parasol Cart
- Liberty Square Portrait Gallery
- Memento Mori
- Ye Olde Christmas Shoppe

ADVENTURELAND

- Agrabah Bazaar
- Bwana Bob's
- Island Supply
- La Princesa de Cristal
- Plaza del Sol Caribe Bazaar
- The Pirates League
- Zanzibar Trading Co.

FRONTIERLAND

- Big Al's
- Briar Patch
- Frontier Trading Post
- Prairie Outpost & Supply
- Splashdown Photos

➪ Main Street USA shops often open earlier and stay open later than regular park hours
➪ There are also various carts and stands that sell souvenirs

A Very Pressing Matter

Pressed coins are one of the most popular souvenirs in Magic Kingdom—and one of the cheapest! Pop in your money and out comes your coin **smushed** into an oval shape with an image on one side. Most of the coin press machines flatten **pennies** but some are for **dimes or quarters**—dimes being the most rare. Coin press machines can usually be found in and around shops but are in **other spots** too like the Fire Station and the Main Street USA train station. Each location offers a choice of **different designs**. People have actually been collecting pressed coins since the **1893 Chicago World's Fair**!

HOT TIP: Pennies made after **1982** have a zinc core and may create a pressed penny with **silver streaks!**

SPY: Looking for one of the rare **dime** press machines? Check in **Tomorrowland Light & Power Co.**

Say "Cheese!"

Talented **PhotoPass photographers** are stationed throughout Magic Kingdom to take pictures of Guests with **characters** and in **scenic spots**. They can snap a **standard** photo or you can request a **Magic Shot** where characters appear in the image **after** it's been taken. You can buy these photos at **Box Office Gifts** in Main Street USA, on the **My Disney Experience** app or from the **Walt Disney World website**. PhotoPass photos are automatically taken **as you ride** on:

- Buzz Lightyear's Space Ranger Spin
- Space Mountain
- Pirates of the Caribbean
- Splash Mountain
- Seven Dwarfs Mine Train

On some rides, your photos will link to your account if you have a **MagicBand**. For others, you can link the photos to your account yourself in the **photo preview area** at the ride's exit.

HOT TIP: PhotoPass photographers are also happy to take photos with **your own camera**.

★ Top 6 Shops

Have fun looking for the perfect souvenir—or just looking!

#1 Main Street Confectionery

What's a confectionery? A candy store! This **Main Street USA** shop hits the sweet spot with Guests. Dotted here and there are copper contraptions, funnels and dials that look like antique candy-making machines. Ornate white shelves and bins trimmed with pretty pastel colors are filled with packaged treats, and glass cases along the wall display the fresh goodies made daily by the confectionery's candy makers.

HOT TIP: Peek into the shop's **candy kitchen** to see what treats are being made that day.

#2 Castle Couture

This charming boutique tucked behind Cinderella Castle in **Fantasyland** features dainty painted flowers, fancy columns and ornate golden woodwork. In this setting fit for a royal dressmaker, you'll find Cinderella's pink dress and Sleeping Beauty's color-changing gown on display.

SPY: Notice the details on the outside of the building like **pin cushions, spools of thread** and other **sewing supplies**.

#3 Mickey's Star Traders

There are a few rides in Magic Kingdom that exit through a gift shop but only one gift shop with a ride going through it! Look up to spot PeopleMovers zipping by inside this **Tomorrowland** shop outfitted with spacey shelving, a glowing constellation of globe lights and retro-futuristic murals topping the walls.

#4 Memento Mori

Nestled just outside Haunted Mansion, this spooky shop in **Liberty Square** gets its name from a tombstone inside the ride's graveyard scene. Dark woodwork, spider web-shaped shelves, and rows of dusty books and candelabras create a moody atmosphere for Haunted Mansion wares.

SPY: **Mysteries** unfold in Memento Mori! Watch the **mirrors** and **paintings** and keep your ears peeled.

HEY KIDS COLOR ME IN!

> SO YOU KNOW...
> **memento mori** = Latin for "remember death," a phrase and type of Victorian art that reminds people that life is short

#5 Plaza del Sol Caribe Bazaar

Pillage and plunder among the pirate loot in the **Adventureland** shop at the exit of Pirates of the Caribbean. An open courtyard is surrounded by nooks and crannies to explore. Treasure maps stuck to the wall with daggers and shelves loaded down with old books, flags and treasure chests fill the shop, whose name is Spanish for "Plaza of the Caribbean Sun Marketplace."

#6 Briar Patch

Br'er Rabbit loves hanging around the Briar Patch and so will you! This cozy **Frontierland** shop near Splash Mountain looks like it's dug right into the red clay hillside. Inside, roots and thorns twist all around the ceiling above a rustic stone fireplace.

SPY: See if you can find **Br'er Rabbit's** family portraits and rabbit-eared furniture.

45

★ Top 4 Rest Spots

#1 Tangled Rest Area

When you've got to go, you've GOT to go to the *Tangled* rest area next to It's a Small World! The buildings feature gorgeous hand-painted artwork, and lanterns and banners decorated with the Kingdom of Corona sun. You'll find Rapunzel's tower, a bubbling brook and a seating area made of barrels and logs.

LOCATION: Fantasyland

"Fine! I'll take you to see the lanterns."
—FLYNN RIDER

SPY: Look for hoofprints left by **Maximus the Horse,** Wanted Posters featuring **Snuggly Duckling ruffians** and ten pals of **Pascal the Chameleon** hiding all around the area.

#2 Hub Grass

The grassy lawns in Central Plaza are a wonderful place to kick back and enjoy the view. Bring a blanket or towel to sit on or just plop yourself right down on the grass.

LOCATION: Main Street USA

#3 Yellow Tent

Step right up to this striped tent in Storybook Circus and take a seat until it's time for your next act.

LOCATION: Fantasyland

SPY: Check out the cute **circus posters** in and around the tent.

#4 Waterfront Gazebo

Hop on a raft to Tom Sawyer Island to discover a covered picnic spot that looks out over the Rivers of America—the perfect place to hang out before or after exploring the island.

LOCATION: Frontierland

Creative Outlets

Picture this...you go to take a photo on a phone or camera and the battery is as **dead as a doornail!** Magic Kingdom has got you covered with convenient **power outlets** that you can use for free.

FANTASYLAND
- Built into logs in the **Tangled rest area**
- Inside the yellow tent in **Storybook Circus**

TOMORROWLAND
- Near the seating area inside **Tomorrowland Light & Power Co.**

You may also find **random outlets** in various restaurants and other shops.

TANGLED CHARACTER QUIZ!

How **well** do you know these *Tangled* characters? Write their name in the **box** connected to their **image**. The first one's been done for you.

Answers on page 191.

Rapunzel

The Story of Tangled

In the Kingdom of Corona, Mother Gothel kidnaps the King and Queen's baby daughter Rapunzel and locks her in a tower so that she can use the magic power found in the princess's hair. Growing up with Pascal the Chameleon as her only friend, Rapunzel passes the time painting, playing guitar and brushing her *very* long hair. Each year on their missing daughter's birthday, her real parents release glowing lanterns into the night sky. Rapunzel doesn't know that she's a princess or what the lanterns are for but yearns to leave the tower and see them up close. Meanwhile Flynn Rider, a common thief (and star of Wanted Posters where they just can't get his nose right) steals Rapunzel's crown from inside the kingdom and happens to try to hideout in Rapunzel's tower. Rapunzel whacks him with a frying pan, ties him up and hides the crown. The two make a deal: Rapunzel will give Flynn back the crown if he takes her to see the lanterns in person. First stop: the Snuggly Duckling pub where Rapunzel is at first frightened by Hookhand, Shorty, Vladimir, Ulf and the other thugs. Once she tells them about her dream, they break into song about their dreams to be a concert pianist, ceramic unicorn collector, mime and more. Throughout their journey, Rapunzel and Flynn are chased by Maximus the Horse from Corona's Royal Army, Mother Gothel, and the Stabbington Brothers who Flynn had double-crossed. Flynn learns that Rapunzel has magic, healing hair and Rapunzel learns that Flynn's real name is Eugene Fitzherbert and that the lanterns are in honor of Corona's lost princess. After the two see the lanterns together and discover they've fallen in love, Mother Gothel tricks Rapunzel and takes her back to the tower. Once there, Rapunzel realizes she is the lost princess. When Flynn comes searching for Rapunzel, the couple defeat Mother Gothel, return to Corona and find the King and the Queen to give them the good news.

Magic Kingdom is the only Disney park to have a Liberty Square.

Main Street USA

What Will You Find in This Chapter?

ATTRACTIONS
- Main Street Vehicles
- Walt Disney World Railroad

ENTERTAINMENT
- Casey's Corner Pianist
- Citizens of Main Street
- Flag Retreat
- Let the Magic Begin
- Main Street Philharmonic
- Main Street Trolley Show
- Mickey's Royal Friendship Faire
- The Dapper Dans

FOOD & DRINKS
- Casey's Corner
- Main Street Bakery
- Plaza Ice Cream Parlor
- The Crystal Palace
- The Plaza Restaurant
- Tony's Town Square Restaurant

MEET N' GREETS
- Classic Characters
- Mickey Mouse
- Tinker Bell

ACTIVITIES, GAMES & INFO
- Terrific Town Square
- Cast a Spell for Fun
- Imagineers at Play
- A Variety of Vehicles!
- Disney Legend Close-up: Blaine Gibson
- Main Street Window Honors
- Who Shops Where?
- Sample Souvenirs
- This Way, That Way, Yonder!

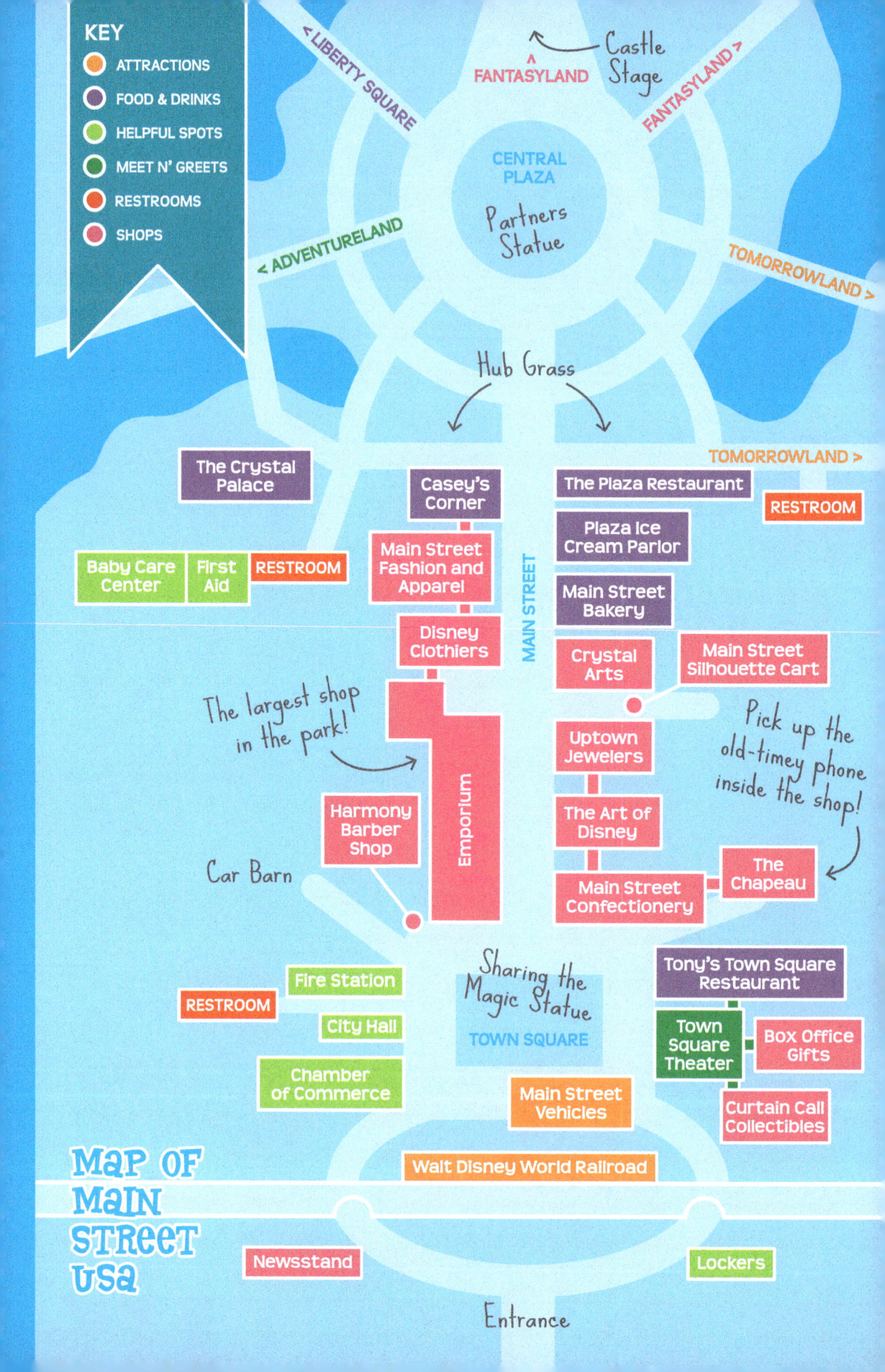

MAP OF MAIN STREET USA

KEY
- ATTRACTIONS
- FOOD & DRINKS
- HELPFUL SPOTS
- MEET N' GREETS
- RESTROOMS
- SHOPS

< LIBERTY SQUARE

FANTASYLAND ^ — Castle Stage

FANTASYLAND >

CENTRAL PLAZA — Partners Statue

< ADVENTURELAND

TOMORROWLAND >

Hub Grass

TOMORROWLAND >

- The Crystal Palace
- Casey's Corner
- The Plaza Restaurant
- RESTROOM
- Baby Care Center
- First Aid
- RESTROOM
- Main Street Fashion and Apparel
- Plaza Ice Cream Parlor
- Main Street Bakery
- MAIN STREET
- Disney Clothiers
- Crystal Arts
- Main Street Silhouette Cart

The largest shop in the park! → Emporium

Pick up the old-timey phone inside the shop! → The Chapeau

- Uptown Jewelers
- Harmony Barber Shop
- The Art of Disney
- Car Barn
- Main Street Confectionery

Sharing the Magic Statue

TOWN SQUARE

- RESTROOM
- Fire Station
- City Hall
- Chamber of Commerce
- Main Street Vehicles
- Tony's Town Square Restaurant
- Town Square Theater
- Box Office Gifts
- Curtain Call Collectibles

Walt Disney World Railroad

- Newsstand
- Lockers

Entrance

> "Aw, come on kid. Start building some memories."
> —TRAMP

Made With a Magical Plan

When you enter Magic Kingdom, the first **world** you'll experience is that of yesterday. **Main Street, USA** is just like a perfect American town from the turn of the century. This land starts off with **Town Square,** a large open area that leads to Main Street. This lovely lane lined with shops and restaurants ends at **Central Plaza** which has paths leading to other lands. To travel between Town Square and Central Plaza, you can either stroll down **Main Street** or hop on an old-timey vehicle. To reach **other lands,** you can catch a train at Main Street station. Whichever way you go, you'll be heading straight for **good times!**

SPY: As you walk through the **tunnels** leading from the entrance to Town Square, be sure to notice the awesome **attraction posters** on display.

I'm glad of that.

Waiting Game!

THE GLAD GAME

In 1960, Disney's *Pollyanna* hit theaters. Pollyanna was a cheerful girl who played the Glad Game where she'd think of something good about something bad. To play, the first player says something bad like, "We just missed that train." Then the next player finds the bright side and says something good like, "But now we can watch The Dapper Dans." Players continue, taking turns in order as long as they like.

51

★ Terrific Town Square

Chamber of Commerce

This building is home to the park's Package Pickup Service. Here Cast Members will happily hold onto your souvenirs so you don't have to straddle that bag of fragile glass figurines as you careen around Big Thunder Mountain! You can have items sent here from various shops in the park and pick them up on your way out.

HOT TIP Pop into the Chamber of Commerce for a **free pinback button** for special occasions like your **Birthday** or **First Visit**. You can also ask for these free buttons in **shops** all over the park.

★ Meet n' Greets

Town Square Theater is home to two indoor places to meet characters. Visit magical Mickey Mouse in his dressing room or step through a portal to Pixie Hollow to make friends with Tinker Bell.

You'll also find classic characters like Chip 'n Dale and Pluto here and there around Town Square.

City Hall

There are two Guest Relations locations—this one and one just outside the entrance—where you can get help with anything from show times to dining reservations to tours and more.

SPY See if you can find photos of Walt Disney World's **"Founding Fathers"** inside City Hall.

Fire Station

Most every town in America has a firehouse and Main Street USA is no different. Engine Co. 71 is named after the year Magic Kingdom opened—1971.

SPY Look around the Fire Station to see **firefighter's patches** from all across America.

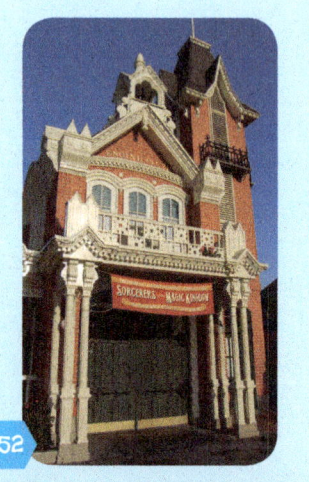

Cast a Spell for Fun

Step inside the Fire Station to enlist in **Sorcerers of the Magic Kingdom**. In this free interactive adventure, you'll help **Merlin the Magician** from *The Sword in the Stone* battle villains—like **Hades** of *Hercules*—throughout the park. You'll get a special **map**, a **key card**, a pack of **spell cards** and **training** from a Cast Member. To play, tap your key card to the keyhole on a **magic portal** to activate it and then defeat the villains who appear using your **spell cards**.

★ That's Entertainment

Mickey Mouse and friends get the day started in front of Cinderella Castle at the Opening Ceremony *Let the Magic Begin.* This is also where to find *Mickey's Royal Friendship Faire,* a live musical stage show.

Throughout the day in various locations, don't miss the colorful antics of the *Citizens of Main Street* and barbershop quartet singing by *The Dapper Dans.* During the *Main Street Trolley Show* performers dance and sing a medley of old-fashioned tunes. At the end of Main Street, catch dazzling piano playing by the *Casey's Corner Pianist.*

Each evening in Town Square, the American flag is lowered and presented to a visiting veteran at the *Flag Retreat* ceremony as the *Main Street Philharmonic* plays patriotic music. You can also see this talented band in Fantasyland playing a mix of big band, ragtime and swing-style Disney classics.

Imagineers at Play

Future plans for Main Street USA include a **new theater** where **live musical shows** will take place. The new venue will be inspired by the **Willis Wood Theater** in Kansas City, Missouri—a town where **Walt Disney** once lived.

So, what do **you** think? Would you like to go to this theater once it opens?
■ Absolutely!   ■ Hmm, maybe…   ■ No way, no how!

RATE THIS ATTRACTION
- ☐ Never. Again.
- ☐ Not so hot.
- ☐ Pretty cool...
- ☐ Way cool!
- ☐ Awesome!!
- ☐ AHH, MY FAVE!!!

One word I'd use to describe this attraction:
_____

FUN FACT
Walt Disney loved trains so much he had one in his own backyard in Los Angeles that was 1/8th the size of a full-size train! Today, you can visit Walt's actual train barn at its new location in L.A.'s Griffith Park.

NEATO!

FANTASYLAND
FRONTIERLAND
MAIN STREET USA

★ Walt Disney World Railroad

steam-train Ride — est. 1971 — calm & mellow

All aboard for a relaxing trip around the park on a classic steam train! Three stations circle the park—one in **Main Street USA,** one in Frontierland and one in Fantasyland. You can hop on for a stop or two, or take the **Grand Circle Tour** to end up back where you started. The trains usually arrive every **five to ten** minutes so you shouldn't have to wait long. Each of the trains is pulled by a real, antique **locomotive engine.** Back in 1969, Imagineer Roger E. Broggie led a team to recover the train engines in Mexico, restore them and create **replicas** of the original passenger cars for Guests to ride in—in **Style!**

HOT TIP: Only strollers that **fold up** are allowed on the train—and they **must be** folded up!

SO YOU KNOW... replicas = copies

SPY: Look around the **Main Street train station** for **signs** that tell all about the history of each of the four trains.

Put a ✓ next to the trains you rode on:
- ☐ Lilly Belle—named after Walt's wife
- ☐ Roger E. Broggie—named after the Imagineer
- ☐ Roy O. Disney—named after Walt's brother
- ☐ Walter E. Disney—named after Walt himself

TIME MACHINE

1916 — Baldwin Locomotive Works of Philadelphia builds the oldest of the Walt Disney World Railroad's engines.

1971 — The train is an Opening Day attraction in Magic Kingdom with Main Street USA as the only station.

1972 — Frontierland station opens & relocates about twenty years later to make room for Splash Mountain. Mighty neighborly!

1988 — Mickey's Birthdayland station opens & is renamed Fantasyland station in 2012.

Main Street Station

Shoeshine Stand – just for looks!

Antique Locks & Keys

A Sorcerers of the Magic Kingdom Portal

Antique Amusements

RATE THIS ATTRACTION
- ☐ Never. Again.
- ☐ Not so hot.
- ☐ Pretty cool...
- ☐ Way cool!
- ☐ Awesome!!
- ☐ AHH, MY FAVE!!!

One word I'd use to describe this attraction:

_____

FUN FACT
When they're not working, the handsome Belgian & Percheron horses that pull the Horse-Drawn Streetcar live at Tri-Circle-D Ranch in Walt Disney World's Fort Wilderness Campground.

NICE!

CENTRAL PLAZA
MAIN STREET
TOWN SQUARE
ENTRANCE

★ Main Street Vehicles

Ah-ooo-gah! Vintage vehicles will take you on a one-way trip up or down Main Street between *Town Square* and *Central Plaza* in front of Cinderella Castle. They all follow the *same route* but pick up and drop off at slightly different spots.

OLD-FASHIONED VEHICLES — EST. 1971 — CALM & MELLOW

HOT TIP: The Main Street Vehicles **do not run** during parades, after dark or when the park is crowded.

Put a ✓ next to the vehicles you rode in:

- ☐ **Fire Engine:** 1910s-style Fire Truck  
- ☐ **Omnibus:** 1920s-style Double-Decker Bus
- ☐ **Jitney/Horseless Carriage:** 1900s-style Car 
- ☐ **Horse-Drawn Streetcar:** 1800s-style Horse-Powered Trolley

a Variety of Vehicles!

There are many different—and **FUN**—ways to move in Magic Kingdom. Draw a line connecting the **ride vehicle** with its **attraction** below. The first one's been done for you. *Answers on page 191.*

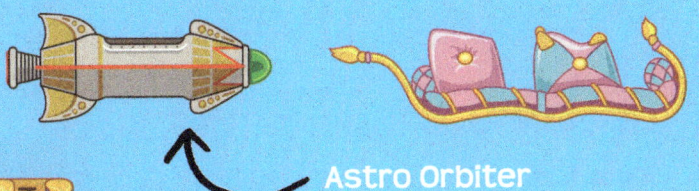

Astro Orbiter
Buzz Lightyear's Space Ranger Spin
Dumbo the Flying Elephant
Haunted Mansion
Mad Tea Party
Peter Pan's Flight
The Magic Carpets of Aladdin
The Many Adventures of Winnie the Pooh
Tomorrowland Speedway

Disney Legend Close-Up: Blaine Gibson

Blaine Gibson was born in Colorado in 1918. He loved to draw and sculpt, and at age 12 he won a **national art contest** for his carving from a bar of soap. In his 20s, Blaine took an art test by mail to get his job in the **animation department** at the Walt Disney Studios where he worked on *Bambi*, *Peter Pan* and *One Hundred and One Dalmatians* to name a few. When Walt Disney saw an exhibit of sculptures Blaine had created in his spare time, he asked Blaine to transfer over to **Imagineering** to help get Disneyland ready for Opening Day. Blaine created hundreds of sculptures for **Audio-Animatronic** figures including those in Pirates of the Caribbean, Haunted Mansion and Enchanted Tiki Room. Later, he worked on Disney attractions for the **1964 World's Fair** including Carousel of Progress, Great Moments with Mr. Lincoln and It's a Small World. Blaine was the **main sculptor** for Magic Kingdom's The Hall of Presidents. You can also see three of his statues around the park—**Cinderella Fountain, Sharing the Magic** and **Partners** which features Walt Disney with Mickey Mouse. Blaine was named a Disney Legend in **1993**.

57

DID YOU EAT IN MAIN STREET USA?
☐ Yes ☐ No
If yes, where?
_____
What'd ya have?
_____
_____
_____
Was it good?
☐ Yes ☐ No
☐ Maybe So

FUN FACT
You can sometimes hear sounds—like a dentist's drill, singing lessons & someone taking a shower—coming from the upstairs windows on a little side lane off Main Street between Main Street Bakery & Uptown Jewelers.

★ Food & Drinks

1888

CASEY'S CORNER
Ballpark favorites are up at bat at this corner spot. Striped wallpaper, stained glass lights and baseball memorabilia bring back the days of 1888 when the poem *Casey at the Bat* was written by Ernest Thayer.
- Corn dog nuggets
- Hot dogs
- Mac n' cheese

MAIN STREET BAKERY
With gleaming brass light fixtures and a pressed tin ceiling, this lively café is a quick stop for a snack on the go.
- Coffee
- Pastries
- Smoothies

The Story of Casey at the Bat

Casey at the Bat was part of Disney's *Make Mine Music* movie from 1946 which was made up of several short cartoons. Casey is the star player of a baseball team in Mudville called the Mudville Nine. With one inning left, the bases are loaded and it's mighty Casey's turn to hit. The pitcher throws the ball but over-confident Casey doesn't even swing for it, saying that one wasn't his style. Strike one! When the next pitch flies, Casey passes on that ball as well. Strike two! Now, the pressure is on. It's Casey's last chance to win the game. The pitch is thrown, but, let's put it this way, there is "no joy in Mudville."

"You're just in time for a little smackerel of something."
—WINNIE THE POOH

Plaza Ice Cream Parlor

With a snazzy black-and-white checkered floor and pale pink and baby blue woodwork, this is a sweet place to satisfy your sweet tooth.
- *Ice cream cones*
- *Ice cream cookie sandwiches*
- *Ice cream sundaes*

HOT TIP Plaza Ice Cream Parlor features a **Flavor of the Month.**

The Crystal Palace

Enjoy dining with Winnie the Pooh and his friends at this restaurant inspired by the elegant greenhouses popular in the Victorian era. Glass-domed ceilings, dramatic windows and hanging plants create a splendid setting for sampling the delights of an all-you-care-to-enjoy buffet.
- *Carved meats* • *Eggs* • *Pancakes*
- *Peel n' eat shrimp*

SPY Many of the park's buildings have **lightning rods** on top which protect the structures from **lightning strikes.** Some are plain while others look like **antennas, weather vanes** or **flagpoles.**

We made some new friends!

Main Street Window Honors

The signs on the windows in Main Street USA honor **real people** who retired after doing exceptional work for Magic Kingdom as artists, carpenters, designers, executives, landscapers, sculptors, writers and more. The windows have people's **names** and made-up **jobs** and/or **companies** related to what they did for the park or their hobby. Look around and you'll see there are many **Main Street Window Honors.** Like to know more? The book *Main Street Windows* by Jeff Heimbuch tells the tale behind the windows in many Disney parks!

59

The Plaza Restaurant

Ready to dine in turn-of-the-century splendor? Fancy **Art Nouveau** mirrored walls and swirly-whirly light fixtures create an elegant setting.
- *Cakes*
- *Cheeseburgers*
- *Meatloaf*
- *Sandwiches*
- *Pies*

> SO YOU KNOW... **Art Nouveau** = decorative style popular around 1900 inspired by the shapes of plants and flowers

Tony's Town Square Restaurant

After you enjoy watching a bit of *Lady and the Tramp* in the waiting area, head into Tony's to feast upon Italian favorites. Handsome dark woodwork, cozy booths and a fountain featuring the famous dog duo set the stage for a *bella notte* (beautiful night)—or *giornata* (day).
- Pastas • Pizza • Salads • Soups

HOT TIP: Ask a Cast Member if they can take your **book** in the back to be signed by Lady and Tramp.

SPY: Look on the **ground** outside of Tony's to find Lady and Tramp's **pawprints!**

The Story of Lady & the Tramp

Lady, a pampered cocker spaniel dog, loves her human family Jim Dear and Darling but worries about her place in the family when their new baby arrives. Aunt Sarah comes to babysit with her naughty cats who cause trouble that Lady gets blamed for. When Lady runs away, a stray mutt named Tramp shows her how he lives a carefree life and the pair enjoy a romantic spaghetti dinner in an alley behind Tony's Restaurant. Lady is caught by a dogcatcher who calls Aunt Sarah to come pick her up. Once Lady is home, Tramp comes to visit and they kill a rat who has snuck into the nursery. Thinking the dogs were trying to attack the baby, Aunt Sarah locks Lady in the basement and calls the dogcatcher to pick up Tramp. When Jim Dear and Darling return and realize what really happened, they treat Lady like a hero and adopt Tramp into their family.

WHO SHOPS WHERE?

Which Disney character might shop in which of these **fake stores**? Draw a line connecting the character's **name** with their **shopping bag**. The first one's been done for you. *Answers on page 191.*

Aladdin
Aladdin, 1992

Jessie
Toy Story 2, 1999

Judy Hopps
Zootopia, 2016

Maui
Moana, 2016

Mulan
Mulan, 1998

Pocahontas
Pocahontas, 1995

Prince Phillip
Sleeping Beauty, 1959

Sally
The Nightmare Before Christmas, 1993

Tarzan
Tarzan, 1999

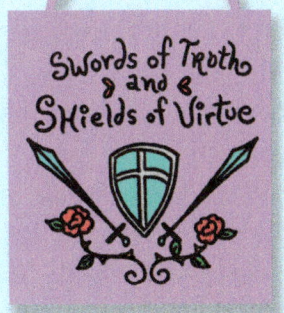

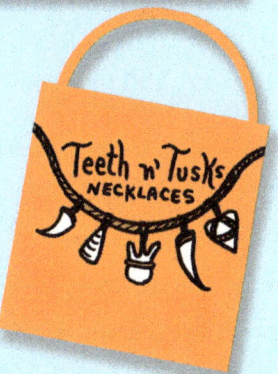

Shopping bags:

- **Princely Turbans** — She'll never guess you're a street rat
- **Cowgirl Cuties** — Yeeee eehaw
- **Land of Loincloths**
- **Halloweentown Sewing Supplies**
- **Perfect Bride Hair Combs**
- **Colors of the Wind Art Supplies**
- **Carrot-Shaped Stuff** — Pens are our specialty!
- **Swords of Truth and Shields of Virtue**
- **Teeth n' Tusks Necklaces**

"So, what do you want with my hair? To cut it?"
—RAPUNZEL

★ Sample Souvenirs

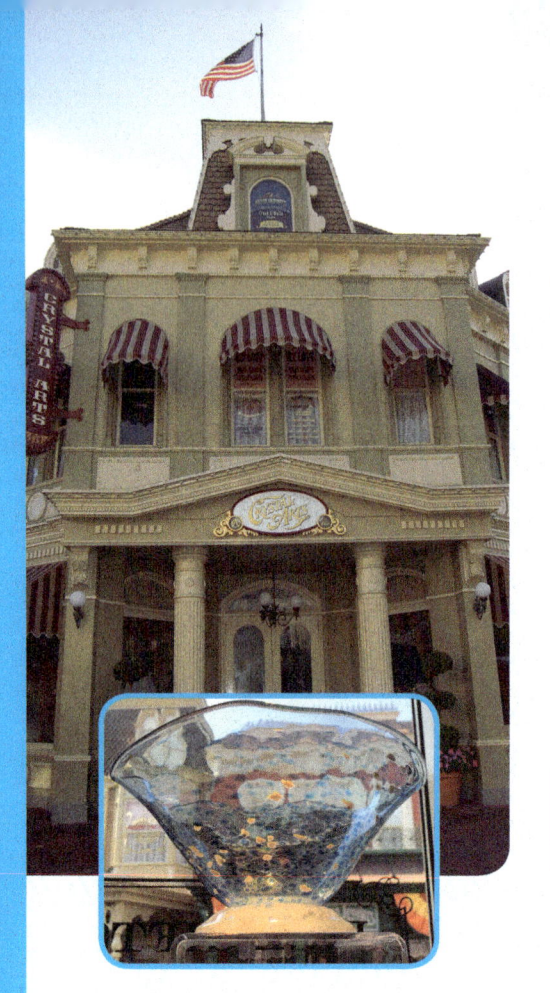

Hand-Blown Glass

Back in 1964, Walt Disney met the Arribas Brothers at the New York World's Fair where the duo were demonstrating their glassblowing skills. After Walt invited them to open a shop in Disneyland, the company went on to open several more in Disney resorts all around the world including **Crystal Arts** in Magic Kingdom. Head to the back of the shop to watch a talented glassblower creating one-of-a-kind collectibles in a real, working furnace.

HOT TIP Crystal Arts also has pre-made glass souvenirs that can be **engraved** with your name or initials while you watch.

Kiddo's First Haircut

Haircuts might be the last thing you'd bother with on a vacation but you may want to think again! At **Harmony Barber Shop** their specialty is making a child's first haircut a truly memorable experience. For about the price of a regular haircut somewhere else, you also get a mouse ear hat, a souvenir certificate for "Bravely and Cheerfully submitting to our Clippers and Shears" and a little pouch to save that first snip of hair. The cheery stylists make the experience lots of fun with stickers, bubbles and toys. Reservations are recommended but walk-ins—and older kids and grownups—are welcome too.

HOT TIP Pop into **Harmony Barber Shop** to ask about getting **FREE pixie dust** sprinkled in your hair!

SPY Next door to Harmony Barber Shop is the **Car Barn**. If the doors are open, peek in to see where the **horses** and **vehicles** go when they're not out and about.

This Way, That Way, Yonder!

Search up and down **Main Street USA** to find these charming sights. Put a ✓ in the box next to the ones you find.

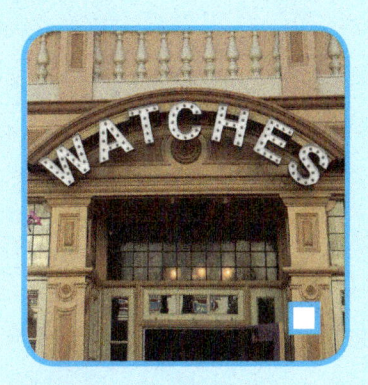

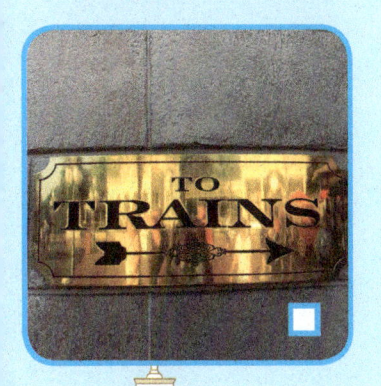

The spectacular Main Street Confectionery is "the home of distinctive treats."

FantasyLand

What Will You Find in This Chapter?

ATTRACTIONS
- Dumbo the Flying Elephant
- Enchanted Tales with Belle
- It's a Small World
- Mad Tea Party
- Mickey's PhilharMagic
- Peter Pan's Flight
- Prince Charming Regal Carrousel
- Seven Dwarfs Mine Train
- The Barnstormer
- The Many Adventures of Winnie the Pooh
- Under the Sea ~ Journey of The Little Mermaid
- Walt Disney World Railroad

ENTERTAINMENT
- Main Street Philharmonic
- The Royal Majesty Makers

FOOD & DRINKS
- Be Our Guest
- Cheshire Café
- Cinderella's Royal Table
- Gaston's Tavern
- Pinocchio Village Haus
- Prince Eric's Village Market
- Storybook Treats
- The Friar's Nook

MEET N' GREETS
- *Alice in Wonderland* characters
- Ariel
- Cinderella
- *Cinderella* characters
- Daisy Duck
- Donald Duck
- Elena of Avalor
- Gaston
- Goofy
- Merida
- Minnie Mouse
- Peter Pan
- Rapunzel
- Tiana
- *Winnie the Pooh* characters

ACTIVITIES, GAMES & INFO
- The Crown Jewel
- Prince Primer
- Phony Baloney!
- Say What? Attraction Edition!
- Oh, Pooh!
- The Shape of Who?
- Spin n' Point!
- Sample Souvenirs
- Disney Legend Close-up: Dorothea Redmond
- This Way, That Way, Yonder!

65

MAP OF FANTASYLAND

KEY
- ATTRACTIONS
- FOOD & DRINKS
- HELPFUL SPOTS
- MEET N' GREETS
- RESTROOMS
- SHOPS

TOMORROWLAND >

STORYBOOK CIRCUS

- Casey Jr. RailRoad Mercantile
- RESTROOM
- Walt Disney World Railroad
- The Barnstormer
- FastPass+ Kiosk (Yellow Tent)
- Pete's Silly Sideshow
- Big Top Souvenirs
- Dumbo the Flying Elephant
- Casey Jr. Splash Pad
- Ariel's Grotto
- Under the Sea ~ Journey of The Little Mermaid
- Bonjour Village Gifts
- RESTROOM
- Prince Eric's Village Market
- Hundred Acre Goods
- The Many Adventures of Winnie the Pooh
- Mad Tea Party
- Cheshire Café
- Seven Dwarfs Mine Train
- Storybook Treats
- RESTROOM
- Fairytale Garden
- Gaston's Tavern
- Be Our Guest
- Castle Wall
- The Friar's Nook
- Princess Fairytale Hall
- Sir Mickey's
- Enchanted Tales with Belle
- RESTROOM
- Pinocchio Village Haus
- Prince Charming Regal Carrousel
- FastPass+ Kiosk
- Castle Couture
- Cinderella's Royal Table
- Bibbidi Bobbidi Boutique
- MAIN STREET USA v
- MAIN STREET USA v
- Cinderella Castle
- Tangled Rest Area
- It's a Small World
- Fantasy Faire
- Mickey's PhilharMagic
- RESTROOM
- LIBERTY SQUARE v
- Peter Pan's Flight
- < LIBERTY SQUARE
- TOMORROWLAND v

"This is the day your dreams come true."
—GASTON

Enchantment Awaits

Fairytales come true in Fantasyland! Glorious Cinderella Castle makes a grand entrance to this land where scenes from your favorite storybooks spring to life. Regal crown-topped tents, arched stone walls and a **Tudor**-style village create a charming setting fit for royalty. This is Magic Kingdom's largest land and features one of the park's newest and most beloved rides—the Seven Dwarfs Mine Train!

HOT TIP Though you'll see a sign overhead as you enter **Storybook Circus**, it's still part of Fantasyland.

SO YOU KNOW...
Tudor = building style with wood timbers, plaster walls, steep roofs and tall windows

I went to school today!

Waiting Game!

TWO JIMINYS AND A PINOCCHIO

In Disney's movie *Pinocchio* from 1940, Jiminy Cricket tells the truth but Pinocchio gets into all kinds of trouble by telling lies. To play, the first player says two things about themselves that are true and one that is a lie. The statements can be in any order. The player could say: "One: I've never eaten an egg. Two: I once rode a camel in France. Three: My favorite color is blue." The other players decide which one they think is the lie and make their guesses, for example: "Number two is the Pinocchio." Once everyone has guessed, the first player reveals the correct answer. Players continue, taking turns in order as long as they like.

"They can't order me to stop dreaming."
—CINDERELLA

The Crown Jewel

Inspired by the **grand palaces** of Europe, Magic Kingdom's Cinderella Castle is the highest structure in the park at **189** feet tall. In **front**, you'll find grassy lawns and blooming flowers while the **rear** includes a courtyard with Cinderella Fountain. On a side walkway, a wishing well features birds and **animals** from *Cinderella*. The castle itself is home to **Bibbidi Bobbidi Boutique** shop on the ground level, **Cinderella's Royal Table** restaurant on the second floor and **Cinderella Castle Suite** on the third floor—exclusive lodgings that are sometimes available to the public as a contest prize.

From a child's point of view, the crown looks like it's on Cinderella's head

Marvelous Mosaics

In the passageway that goes through the castle, five **tile murals** line one of the walls and tell the tale of Cinderella. Following designs by **Dorothea Redmond,** mosaic artist **Hanns-Joachim Scharff** and his team spent almost two years assembling these incredible mosaics from over **300,000** pieces of colorful Italian glass, sterling silver and **14-karat** gold.

The Story of Cinderella

Sweet Cinderella lives a happy life until her doting father dies, leaving her all alone with her wicked stepmother Lady Tremaine and her two vain stepsisters, Anastasia and Drizella. Treated as a servant in her own home, Cinderella is banished to a lonely attic bedroom with only mice like Jaq, Gus, Suzy, Perla and other animals for friends. When Lady Tremaine refuses to let her go to Prince Charming's ball, Cinderella is heartbroken. Her Fairy Godmother appears and uses the magic words "Bibbidi-Bobbidi-Boo!" to change Cinderella's rags into a beautiful ballgown, a pumpkin into a coach, and animals into footmen. There's just one catch: the magic will wear off at midnight. At the ball, Prince Charming and Cinderella fall deeply in love. As the clock strikes midnight, Cinderella rushes away leaving a single glass slipper behind. Prince Charming searches far and wide for the girl whose foot will fit the shoe. When he finally finds Cinderella, they marry and live happily ever after.

★ Prince Charming Regal Carrousel

Spelled with TWO r's!

RATE THIS ATTRACTION
- ☐ Never. Again.
- ☐ Not so hot.
- ☐ Pretty cool...
- ☐ Way cool!
- ☐ Awesome!!
- ☐ AHH, MY FAVE!!!

One word I'd use to describe this attraction:
_____

Take a spin on a *magnificent* antique carousel! Hand-carved wooden horses prance underneath a colorful *medieval* tent and painted panels that tell the tale of Prince Charming and his sweetheart, Cinderella. Each one of the *horses* is totally *unique* with saddles and bridles decorated with flowers, feathers, jewels, shields and other *delightful* details. During your journey, enjoy the cheerful organ music and see if you hear any songs you recognize!

SPY: Rumor has it that the horse with the **gold ribbon** is **Cinderella's horse.** Find it **three** rows up from the chariot bench, **one** row in from the outer ring.

FUN FACT
The Liberty Carousel was made in 1917 by the Philadelphia Toboggan Company in Pennsylvania, purchased by Imagineers in 1967, restored & turned into what is today Prince Charming Regal Carrousel.

LOVELY!

antique carousel — est. 1971 — calm & mellow

Which carousel horse do you like best?
_____

TIME MACHINE

1697 — "Cendrillon" by Charles Perrault is published & is the most popular version of the Cinderella folktale.

1950 — Bibbidi-Bobbidi-Boo! "Cinderella" hits theaters.

1971 — Cinderella's Golden Carrousel is an Opening Day attraction in Magic Kingdom.

2010 — Cinderella's Golden Carrousel is renamed Prince Charming Regal Carrousel.

Prince Primer

NAME The Prince
FROM *Snow White and the Seven Dwarfs*, 1937
TRUE LOVE Snow White
QUOTE "Wait, wait please. Don't run away!"
CHALLENGE Must search far and wide for his true love who he thinks is dead
WHAT HE'S LIKE Dandy dresser, single-minded, wonderful singer

NAME Charming
FROM *Cinderella*, 1950
TRUE LOVE Cinderella
QUOTE "I don't even know your name. How will I find you?"
CHALLENGE Must marry so his kingdom has a queen
WHAT HE'S LIKE Gracious host, loving son, good at finding missing people

NAME Phillip
FROM *Sleeping Beauty*, 1959
TRUE LOVE Aurora
QUOTE "It wasn't a dream, father. I really did meet her."
CHALLENGE Must battle a fierce dragon to rescue his true love
WHAT HE'S LIKE Skilled warrior, brave in the face of danger, enjoys long rides in the woods

NAME Eric
FROM *The Little Mermaid*, 1989
TRUE LOVE Ariel
QUOTE "She had the most beautiful voice."
CHALLENGE Needs to find the girl he fell in love with on the beach
WHAT HE'S LIKE Enjoys sailing, devoted to his dog, falls in love easily

NAME The Beast
FROM *Beauty and the Beast*, 1991
TRUE LOVE Belle
QUOTE "Oh, it's no use. She's so beautiful and I'm...well, look at me!"
CHALLENGE Must break a curse to be able to turn back into a human
WHAT HE'S LIKE Generous gift giver, has questionable table manners, learns from his mistakes

NAME Naveen
FROM *The Princess and the Frog*, 2009
TRUE LOVE Tiana
QUOTE "Kissing would be nice, yes?"
CHALLENGE He and Tiana have been turned into frogs
WHAT HE'S LIKE Fun-loving and flirtatious, musical, excellent at hopping

RATE THIS ATTRACTION
- ■ Never. Again.
- ■ Not so hot.
- ■ Pretty cool...
- ■ Way cool!
- ■ Awesome!!
- ■ AHH, MY FAVE!!!

One word I'd use to describe this attraction:

_____

FUN FACT
As the story in Mickey's PhilharMagic unfolds, you'll travel to settings from several classic Disney movies—Agrabah, Ariel's Grotto, Peter Pan's London, Simba's Africa & the Beast's Dining Hall. This movie is the first time those places were created in 3D animation.

BRAVO!

★ Mickey's PhilharMagic

INDOOR SHOW — est. 2003 — Lively & exciting

It's showtime! This **3D movie** is shown on a ginormous 150 foot-wide wrap-around screen in Fantasyland Concert Hall. You'll get a pair of **opera glasses** to put on when Minnie Mouse gives the word. As the show begins, **Mickey Mouse** rushes offstage to get ready, leaving behind a magical sorcerer's hat. **Donald Duck** decides to get the show started and puts on the hat to work a little **magic** of his own. As the orchestra's instruments play themselves, things spiral out of control and Donald loses the hat. As he hunts it down, Donald makes his way through a medley of **musical numbers** from *Beauty and the Beast*, *The Lion King*, *Aladdin* and more!

HOT TIP: Mickey's PhilharMagic features **scents** and other **surprises**.

SO YOU KNOW... PhilharMagic = philharmonic (an orchestra) + magic

PHONY BALONEY!

All of these **shows** and **movies** were where Mickey's PhilharMagic is today—except for **one**. Can you put a ✓ next to the fake? *Answer on page 191.*

- ■ Bibbidi Bobbidi Boogie
- ■ Legend of the Lion King
- ■ Magic Journeys
- ■ Mickey Mouse Revue

Say What? Attraction Edition!

Guess which **phrase** can be heard in which **attraction**. Draw a **line** connecting the attraction's **name** with the **quote**. The first one's been done for you. *Answers on page 191.*

- Yeah, we ain't goin' anywhere anyhow.
- Pilots, prepare for lift-off! → Astro Orbiter
- The orchestra's missing and it's showtime!
- Big Thunder Mountain Railroad
- Country Bear Jamboree
- Which offers you this chilling challenge—to find a way out!
- Haunted Mansion
- If any of you folks are wearin' hats or glasses, best remove 'em.
- Mickey's PhilharMagic
- Peter Pan's Flight
- Pirates of the Caribbean
- The Magic Carpets of Aladdin
- Dead men tell no tales…
- Help me, Mr. Smee, help me!
- Then let's fly to Agrabah!

Music You Can See

Music has always been just as important as the **story** in Disney movies but 1940's *Fantasia* is **all about** the music. The movie features eight short cartoons set to pieces of **classical music** by famous composers like Bach, Beethoven and Tchaikovsky. The most well-known of these shorts is *The Sorcerer's Apprentice* where **Mickey Mouse** is a helper to a magician named **Yen Sid** (that's Disney backwards). When his master steps away, Mickey puts on Yen's **magic hat** and tries to cast some spells himself!

RATE THIS ATTRACTION
- ■ Never. Again.
- ■ Not so hot.
- ■ Pretty cool...
- ■ Way cool!
- ■ Awesome!!
- ■ AHH, MY FAVE!!!

One word I'd use to describe this attraction:
_____

FUN FACT
It is rumored that "Peter Pan" author J.M. Barrie ordered Brussels sprouts for lunch every day just because he liked the way the words sounded.

HA!

★ Peter Pan's Flight

Come on everybody, here we go-o-o-o! With the help of some *pixie dust*, you'll fly through the air on a pirate ship from the Darling's nursery in London to the island of Never Land. As Nana the Dog barks below, you'll soar out the window and over the rooftops of the sparkling city past *Big Ben* and *Tower Bridge*. Once you reach Never Land, you'll encounter villainous pirate *Captain Hook* shouting commands at Mr. Smee, mermaids relaxing on rocks and proud *Tiger Lily* having a powwow with her father, the Indian Chief. After Peter Pan battles the Captain, Peter and the *Darling children* set sail for London—but Hook won't be so lucky!

SPY See if you can spot **Raggedy Ann and Andy dolls** on Peter Pan's Flight.

Indoor Dark Ride • est. 1971 • Lively & Exciting

★ Meet n' Greets

Look for *Peter Pan* next to Peter Pan's Flight—unless he's flown back to Never Land!

TIME MACHINE

1904 — J.M. Barrie writes "Peter Pan" after the character is well received in an earlier novel.

1953 — You can fly! "Peter Pan" hits theaters.

1971 — Peter Pan's Flight opens a few days after Magic Kingdom's Opening Day.

2014 — Interactive fun is added to the regular standby line for Peter Pan's Flight.

"Oh, look! A firefly!"
—MICHAEL DARLING

The Story of Peter Pan

While getting ready to go out for the evening, Mr. Darling gets jealous that Mrs. Darling and their children, Wendy, Michael and John, are paying more attention to Nana the Dog than they are to him. He orders Nana outside and tells Wendy it's time for her to grow up and that this will be her last night with her brothers in the nursery. Wendy tries to tell her mother that Peter Pan has been visiting their house and she's captured his shadow, but Mrs. Darling doesn't listen. After the parents leave, Peter and his fairy friend Tinker Bell fly in the window to find Peter's shadow. Peter sprinkles the three children with Tinker Bell's pixie dust, tells them to think happy thoughts and flies with them from London to Never Land—a wondrous place where children never grow up. Never Land is home to the Lost Boys, beautiful mermaids, Native American Indian princess Tiger Lily and her father the Indian Chief, pirates like Captain Hook and his faithful assistant Mr. Smee, and hungry crocodile Tick-Tock—named for the ticking clock he accidentally swallowed. After many exciting adventures in Never Land, the Darling children and the Lost Boys realize they miss their mothers back in London and want to go home but are captured by the pirates. After Hook gets Tinker Bell to reveal Peter's location, he delivers a bomb to Peter, now alone in his secret hideout. Tink saves Peter but almost dies in the explosion. She and Peter defeat the pirates and Hook is chased into the distance by Tick-Tock. Peter takes the Darling children home in a pixie dust-covered pirate ship that Mr. Darling could swear he's seen somewhere before.

Winning Entry by Savanna Rodriguez from the Going To Guides Art Contest!

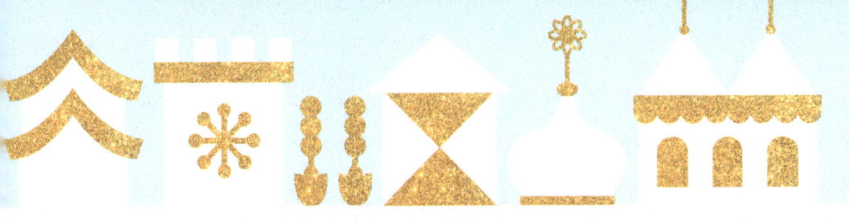

★ It's a Small World

Embark on a lively international adventure! You'll cruise the *Seven Seaways Waterway* through exotic locales including Africa, Antartica, Asia, Australia, Europe, South America, the South Pacific Islands and the Middle East. Along the way dozens of *dolls,* colorfully dressed in the traditional clothing of their homeland, sing the ride's catchy tune in *several* languages. You'll also see *adorable animals* like swaying giraffes, spinning penguins and rocking kangaroos. For the *grand finale,* the children from all of the countries sing together but this time their outfits are mainly white as a symbol of *world peace* and harmony.

Indoor Boat Ride — Calm & Mellow — EST. 1971

SPY See if you can find **one golden sun** in each part of It's a Small World.

RATE THIS ATTRACTION
- ■ Never. Again.
- ■ Not so hot.
- ■ Pretty cool...
- ■ Way cool!
- ■ Awesome!!
- ■ AHH, MY FAVE!!!

One word I'd use to describe this attraction:
_____

FUN FACT
In the 2015 movie "Tomorrowland," a boy at the 1964 World's Fair is given a pin with a T on it & told to ride It's a Small World. When he does, the pin sets off a scanner which causes his boat to enter a futuristic dimension called Tomorrowland.

WOW!

TIME MACHINE

1964
It's a Small World debuts at the New York World's Fair.

1971
There's so much that we share! It's a Small World is an Opening Day attraction in Magic Kingdom.

1994
Zazu sings It's a Small World's theme song in "The Lion King."

2013
"It's a Small World: The Animated Series" begins & features the adventures of six international friends.

RATE THIS ATTRACTION
- ☐ Never. Again.
- ☐ Not so hot.
- ☐ Pretty cool...
- ☐ Way cool!
- ☐ Awesome!!
- ☐ AHH, MY FAVE!!!

One word I'd use to describe this attraction:

_____

FUN FACT
Because Mr. Toad's Wild Ride was an Opening Day attraction in this location, there's a picture of Toadie handing the ownership papers over to Owl in Owl's house.

FUNNY!

MAY BE SCARY

★ The Many Adventures of Winnie the Pooh

INDOOR DARK RIDE ★ EST. 1999 ★ Lively & exciting

Ready to go adventuring with *Pooh?* Hop into a *Hunny Pot* to travel through the pages of a giant storybook to a *blustery* day in Hundred Acre Wood. As Pooh and his friends get blown around by the wind, you'll ride through the *damage* at Owl's house. Next, your Hunny Pot *bounces* up and down merrily with Tigger as he heads to Pooh's house for a visit. When Pooh falls asleep, you'll drift through his *zany dreams* filled with *wildly* colorful Heffalumps and Woozles. Back awake, Pooh—and his friends—are almost washed away by rain but, in the end, the *storm* goes away and everyone says "Hooray!"

SPY Look inside Pooh's hollow tree out front for the shape of the **Nautilus**—a submarine from the now-gone **20,000 Leagues Under the Sea.**

★ Meet n' Greets

There's a place for friends to meet *Winnie the Pooh characters* like Pooh and Tigger next to Pooh's ride.

TIME MACHINE

1926 — The first collection of stories about a 'silly old bear' are published in the book "Winnie-the-Pooh."

1968 — How lucky we are! "Winnie the Pooh & the Blustery Day" hits theaters.

1999 — The Many Adventures of Winnie the Pooh debuts in Magic Kingdom.

2010 — Interactive fun is added to the regular standby line for The Many Adventures of Winnie the Pooh.

OH, POOH!

The **blustery winds** have blown the **letters** in Winnie the Pooh's name all around. How many **words** can you make using these **letters**? It's **okay** to use a letter more than once. The first one's been done for you.

NEPHEW

A little boy named Christopher Robin enjoys adventures in Hundred Acre Wood with Winnie the Pooh and his pals Eeyore, Gopher, Kanga and Roo, Owl, Piglet, Rabbit and Tigger. One day, Gopher warns Pooh that it is "Windsday" but Pooh gets confused and wishes his friends a Happy Windsday. As Piglet tries to sweep, strong winds blow him and Pooh over to Owl's house—which ends up getting wrecked by the wind. That night as the blustery weather continues, Tigger meets Pooh at his house and tells him about strange creatures called Heffalumps (which look sort of like elephants) and Woozles (which look sort of like weasels) who may try to steal Pooh's honey. Pooh is scared and tries to stay awake to guard his honey but eventually falls asleep and has strange nightmares. When Pooh wakes up, the winds have turned into a major storm with heavy rains and flooding that wash him and his friends away. When the weather finally clears, everyone gathers together to have party and celebrate!

The Story of Winnie the Pooh

RATE THIS ATTRACTION
- ☐ Never. Again.
- ☐ Not so hot.
- ☐ Pretty cool...
- ☐ Way cool!
- ☐ Awesome!!
- ☐ AHH, MY FAVE!!!

One word I'd use to describe this attraction:

_____

FUN FACT
Seven Dwarfs Mine Train was the world's first roller coaster with swinging seats that rock side to side depending on which way the track twists & turns.

ROCK ON!

★ Seven Dwarfs Mine Train

MAY BE SCARY

Roller Coaster · est. 2014 · Wild & Thrilling

Heigh-Ho-o-o-o-o! Enjoy a rollicking ride on a **mine train** through the mountain where the dwarfs work. To enter, follow a winding path through a **woodsy** setting to a tunnel that leads inside the mine. Once aboard your train, you'll head back outside and **smoothly** soar and sway up, down and all around the mountain. Next, you'll enter the jewel mine where the dwarfs are collecting glimmering **gemstones** and—of course—**whistling** while they work! Back outside you go, dashing around twists and turns until you pass **Snow White** and the dwarfs dancing and playing music inside their cottage, while **someone** lurks outside!

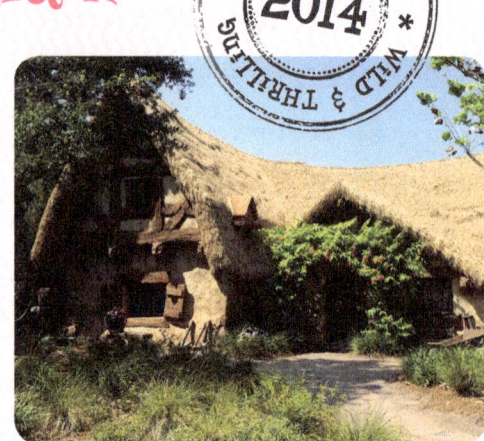

HOT TIP: This is one of a handful of rides in Walt Disney World where you get not just photos but **videos** automatically added to your **PhotoPass** account.

SPY: When you're in the mine, look for a **clock** with two miners carved on top. Just like in the movie, when the clock **chimes** the dwarfs start singing.

TIME MACHINE

1812 — "Snow White" by the Brothers Grimm is published in Germany as "Sneewittchen."

1937 — "Snow White & the Seven Dwarfs" hits theaters.

2012 — Opening Day attraction Snow White's Adventures closes to make room for Princess Fairytale Hall.

2014 — It's off to ride we go! Seven Dwarfs Mine Train debuts in Magic Kingdom.

As the princess Snow White sweetly sings by a wishing well, a handsome prince joins her in song and they fall in love. Snow White's villainous stepmother, the Evil Queen, is jealous of her beauty and orders her huntsman to take Snow White out to the forest and bring back her heart. The huntsman can't bring himself to do the evil deed and tells Snow White to run away into the woods where she finds the cottage of the seven dwarfs— Bashful, Doc, Dopey, Grumpy, Happy, Sleepy and Sneezy. The dwarfs mine for jewels all day and agree to let Snow White stay with them in exchange for cooking and cleaning their cottage. Meanwhile, the Evil Queen learns from her Magic Mirror that Snow White is still alive. The Evil Queen disguises herself as an Old Hag, visits Snow White and tricks her into biting a poisoned apple. Snow White falls into a sleeping death that can only be broken by true love's kiss. The dwarfs return and chase the Evil Queen up a cliff where she is struck by lightning and falls to her death. When the dwarfs return to their cottage and see Snow White, they think she's dead and place her in a glass coffin. The prince comes to pay his respects and everyone is surprised and overjoyed when his kiss awakens her.

The Story of Snow White

RATE THIS ATTRACTION
- ☐ Never. Again.
- ☐ Not so hot.
- ☐ Pretty cool...
- ☐ Way cool!
- ☐ Awesome!!
- ☐ AHH, MY FAVE!!!

One word I'd use to describe this attraction:

_____

FUN FACT
In the 2017 live-action "Beauty & the Beast," the floor in the ballroom features the swirly letters "W" & "D" as a tribute to Walt Disney.

SUPERB!

★ Enchanted Tales with Belle

INDOOR SHOW · EST. 2012 · CALM & MELLOW

Wind down the path to *Maurice's Cottage* to enjoy a visit with Belle and her friends. Inside the cozy dwelling, you'll see stacks of books, rolled-up sketches and Belle's father's *clever* inventions. On the wall hangs a gift from the Beast— a *Magic Mirror* which transforms into a doorway to the Beast's castle. Once inside the Beast's elegant home, Cast Members will introduce you to Madame Wardrobe and Lumiere before they chose members of the *audience* to help act out scenes from *Beauty and the Beast*. When everyone heads into the library, *Belle* joins the gathering and helps to put on the show!

HOT TIP: If you're chosen to be one of the **actors**, you'll have a chance to take a **photo** with Belle and get a **souvenir bookmark** to take to your cottage.

TIME MACHINE

1740 — "La Belle et la Bête" by French author Gabrielle-Suzanne Barbot de Villeneuve is published.

1991 — "Beauty & the Beast" hits theaters.

1999 — The live, interactive show Storytime with Belle takes place in Fairytale Garden until 2010.

2012 — Enchanted Tales with Belle opens. Ooh la la!

"Well, some people use their imagination."
—BELLE

The Story of Beauty & the Beast

Belle lives in a quiet village with her father, the inventor Maurice. She loves to read but does not love stuck-up Gaston, even though he thinks she should. Gaston tells his faithful friend LeFou all about his plan to make Belle his wife, never dreaming she'll say no. Maurice gets lost in the woods and looks for help in an enchanted castle, the home of a cursed prince who's been turned into a hideous beast. The prince must earn someone's love before the last petal falls from an enchanted rose or he will be doomed to stay a beast forever. Inside the castle, Maurice meets the Beast's servants who have been turned into objects as part of the curse—a candlestick (Lumiere), a clock (Cogsworth), a teapot (Mrs. Potts), a teacup (Chip) and others. After tracking down her father, Belle takes his place as the Beast's prisoner. She tries to escape into the woods and the Beast is injured when he saves her from fierce wolves. When Belle tends to his wounds the two become friends—and maybe something more. Knowing she loves to read, the Beast gives Belle his library. When Belle looks in the Beast's enchanted mirror and sees her father is in danger, the Beast lets her leave to help him and gives her the mirror. Back in the village, Maurice tries to tell the others about the Beast but no one will believe him. Gaston, hoping to force Belle to marry him, tries to get "crazy old Maurice" locked up in an insane asylum. Belle arrives in the village and proves her father is right by showing the Beast to Gaston in the mirror. Gaston leads an angry mob to storm the castle and kill the creature. After a fierce battle, Gaston falls to his death from the roof. Belle reaches the dying Beast as the last petal falls from the rose. She tells him, "I love you." and, with those words, the curse is broken and the Beast and his servants become human again.

RATE THIS ATTRACTION
- ☐ Never. Again.
- ☐ Not so hot.
- ☐ Pretty cool...
- ☐ Way cool!
- ☐ Awesome!!
- ☐ AHH, MY FAVE!!!

One word I'd use to describe this attraction:
_____

FUN FACT
Ursula's evil eels are named **Flotsam** & **Jetsam**. **Flotsam** means loose stuff floating in the sea, like after a shipwreck. **Jetsam** means goods thrown overboard to make a ship lighter or more balanced.

OH!

★ Under the Sea ~ Journey of The Little Mermaid

MAY BE SCARY

INDOOR DARK RIDE • est. 2012 • calm & mellow

Visit Prince Eric's *castle* to journey through the *tale* of The Little Mermaid. You'll climb into a *clamshell* and pass Scuttle the Seagull who starts off the story. After you dive under *"da bubbles"* you'll float past Ariel as she sings with Flounder the Fish among her treasures and then enjoys a festive *shindig* with Sebastian the Crab. Things take a dark turn when you reach Ursula's *lair* where she conjures up a *magic spell* to give Ariel legs and steal her voice. Back up on land, Ariel hopes for a *kiss* as she shares a quiet rowboat ride with Prince Eric. When the lovebirds *finally* smooch, the spell is broken and King Triton and all the sea creatures—except Ursula—celebrate Eric and Ariel's *royal wedding!*

SPY — Look among Ariel's treasures to spy a **dinglehopper** balancing on a candelabra.

SO YOU KNOW... **grotto** = watery cavern

★ Meet n' Greets

Swim over to meet mermaid *Ariel* at Ariel's **Grotto** next to her ride.

TIME MACHINE

1837 — The story of The Little Mermaid, "Den Lille Havfrue," by author Hans Christian Andersen, is first published.

1989 — Splash! "The Little Mermaid" hits theaters.

1996 — Ariel's Grotto opens in Magic Kingdom, closes in 2010 & reopens in a new location in 2012.

2012 — Under the Sea ~ Journey of The Little Mermaid opens in Magic Kingdom.

Ariel the Mermaid lives under the sea with her father King Triton and her six sisters but daydreams of living on land. She's friends with Flounder the Fish, Sebastian the Crab and Scuttle the Seagull who she chats with about her collection of objects from the human world. When King Triton sees her treasure trove, he's furious and orders her to stop daydreaming. Ariel returns to the surface where she falls in love with the handsome Prince Eric. She rescues Eric from drowning and sings to him in her angelic voice. When Eric's servant Grimsby and dog Max approach, Ariel rushes away and Eric vows to find her. Yearning for Eric, Ariel visits Ursula the Sea Witch who captures Ariel's voice in a nautilus shell and magically transforms her mermaid tail into legs. Ursula warns Ariel that she only has three days to get Eric to kiss her or Ariel's voice—and soul—will be hers forever. When Eric finds Ariel on the beach, he wonders if she's the mysterious girl who saved him but thinks he must be mistaken when he learns she can't speak. The two grow closer and share a romantic boat ride but Ursula's evil eels Flotsam and Jetsam tip the boat over before Eric can kiss Ariel. Disguising herself as a beautiful woman named Vanessa, Ursula uses Ariel's voice and magic to trick Eric into agreeing to marry her. At last Ariel gets her voice back and Eric wakes from Ursula's spell to realize she's the girl he's been searching for. After a fierce battle between Ursula—who has returned to her Sea Witch form—and King Triton, she is defeated. When King Triton sees how much Ariel truly loves Eric, he uses his powers to make her dream of being human come true.

The Story of The Little Mermaid

RATE THIS ATTRACTION
- ☐ Never. Again.
- ☐ Not so hot.
- ☐ Pretty cool...
- ☐ Way cool!
- ☐ Awesome!!
- ☐ AHH, MY FAVE!!!

One word I'd use to describe this attraction:

_____

FUN FACT
When Dumbo the Flying Elephant was moved to its current location, a second ride was added—now one spins counter-clockwise & the other spins clockwise. Some people joke that these are the Dueling Dumbos.

HA HA!

Which color hat do you like best on Dumbo?

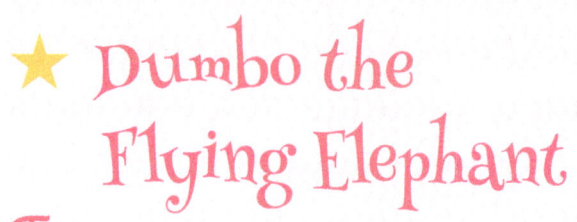

_____

★ Dumbo the Flying Elephant

Flap your ears and fly! Fancy central *columns* are decorated with Mr. Stork making a special delivery, the smiling face of *Mrs. Jumbo* and scenes from story of Dumbo. Below, sparkling fountains spray fans of water and *glow* at night with rainbow-colored lights. A collection of Dumbo *gondolas* circle the column—each one with a different colored hat and blanket. Once you begin to spin, you can control how high you go with a *lever* inside your elephant. As cheery circus music plays, skim down along the water or *soar* up into the skies of Storybook Circus!

Outdoor Spinning Ride • Lively & exciting • est. 1971

HOT TIP: There is an **extra gondola** in front of this attraction that makes an excellent **photo spot**.

SPY: Be sure to look for **Timothy Q. Mouse** on top of the archway leading to his pal Dumbo's ride.

TIME MACHINE

1941 — "Dumbo," created from a 1939 children's story by Helen Aberson, hits theaters.

1971 — Magic Kingdom opens with Dumbo the Flying Elephant as an Opening Day attraction near Pinocchio Village Haus.

1988 — Mickey's Birthdayland opens & later changes to Mickey's Starland, then Mickey's Toyland, then Mickey's Toontown Fair.

2012 — The new Dumbo ride opens inside Storybook Circus, where Mickey's Toontown Fair used to be. Whee!

Walt Disney World Railroad

Fantasyland station in Storybook Circus is one of the three stops on the Walt Disney World Railroad. *More info on page 54.*

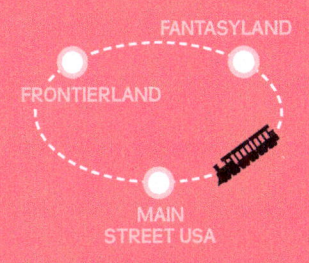

FANTASYLAND
FRONTIERLAND
MAIN STREET USA

SPY The name of Walt Disney's backyard train was **Carolwood Pacific Railroad.** Look around Fantasyland Station to see **how many places** you can find the word "Carolwood" on signs and posters around the station.

The Story of Dumbo

As the Casey Jr. Circus Train arrives in town, a circus elephant named Mrs. Jumbo gets a visit from Mr. Stork who brings her a baby boy. She is delighted with her new child and names him Jumbo, Jr. but the other animals make fun of his huge ears and call him Dumbo. When some mean human kids tease her son, Mrs. Jumbo goes into a rage and is locked up. The little elephant is very sad without his mother but makes friends with a mouse named Timothy Q. Mouse. After a wild night, Timothy and Dumbo wake up in a tall tree and Timothy guesses that Dumbo must have flown them up there. To boost Dumbo's confidence in himself, he gives him a magic feather and tells Dumbo that if he has that, he'll be able to fly. Dumbo believes in the magic, flaps his ears and takes off into the air. Later, when performing at the circus, Dumbo loses the feather and realizes he never needed it to fly anyway—he can do it all on his own! Dumbo becomes famous for his flying skills and is reunited with his mother at last.

RATE THIS ATTRACTION
- ☐ Never. Again.
- ☐ Not so hot.
- ☐ Pretty cool...
- ☐ Way cool!
- ☐ Awesome!!
- ☐ AHH, MY FAVE!!!

One word I'd use to describe this attraction:
_____

FUN FACT
Tall structures around an airfield have a red & white checkered pattern so they can be clearly seen & no one will accidentally crash into them.

OOPS!

★ The Barnstormer

Roller Coaster est. 1996 Lively & exciting

Ready to take off with that famous daredevil *The Great Goofini?* You'll depart from an airplane hanger made from an old barn in a bright red *stunt plane.* As you skyrocket around the barnyard, you'll burst through a checkered *tower* and a *billboard* before coming in for a smooth landing. A trip on The Barnstormer is *short* and *sweet* which makes it a great first roller coaster for kids!

SPY Look for an **awning** made with Goofy's **boxer shorts.**

SO YOU KNOW... barnstormer = pilot who entertains by doing tricks in an airplane

★ Meet n' Greets

Pete's Silly Sideshow next to Big Top Souvenirs is the place to visit with *Minnie Mouse* as poodle trainer "Minnie Magnifique" and *Daisy Duck* as fortuneteller "Daisy Fortuna" on one side or *Donald Duck* as snake charmer "The Astounding Donaldo" and *Goofy* as stuntman "The Great Goofini" on the other.

TIME MACHINE

1932 — Goofy makes his debut in a short cartoon called "Mickey's Revue." Gawrsh!

1995 — Goofy, his son Max & neighbor Pete star in "A Goofy Movie."

1996 — The Barnstormer at Goofy's Wiseacre Farm debuts in Magic Kingdom.

2012 — Now a part of Storybook Circus, Goofy's roller coaster reopens as The Barnstormer.

THE SHAPE OF WHO?

At **The Barnstormer**, you'll see the **shape** of Goofy busted through a bullseye on a **safety net**. Draw a line connecting the **net** below with the **character** who's gone through it. The first one's been done for you. *Answers on page 191.*

Goofy

Jiminy Cricket

Lumiere

Marie

Piglet

Sebastian

The Mad Hatter

Timothy Q. Mouse

RATE THIS ATTRACTION
- ■ Never. Again.
- ■ Not so hot.
- ■ Pretty cool...
- ■ Way cool!
- ■ Awesome!!
- ■ AHH, MY FAVE!!!

One word I'd use to describe this attraction:

_____

FUN FACT

Lewis Carroll thought about calling his most famous book "Alice's Adventures Under Ground," "Alice's Hour in Elf-Land" or "Alice Among the Fairies."

HUH!

★ Mad Tea Party

SO YOU KNOW... topiaries = bushes trimmed into shapes

Outdoor Spinning Ride — est. 1971 — Lively & Exciting

A very merry unbirthday to you! You only have one birthday a year but you have 364 **unbirthdays!** Whichever one you're celebrating, what better way is there to enjoy it than taking a spin in a **teacup**? A wonderland of **topiaries** surround a spiral tea tray topped with a **canopy** decorated with colorful **lanterns**. As the jolly music plays, you'll sit inside an oversized **teacup** and twirl around a tall teapot. You can control if you want to spin even more with a **wheel** in the center of your cup, so get ready to get dizzy!

HOT TIP — While you're waiting for **your turn,** pick out which **color** teacup you want to ride in—though someone **may** get to it before you do!

SPY — Watch for the teapot's **lid** to raise to see the **Dormouse!**

Which color teacup do you like best?

_____

★ Meet n' Greets

If meeting **Alice in Wonderland characters** is your cup of tea, look around Mad Tea Party to see if any of them have popped 'round.

TIME MACHINE

1865 — "Alice's Adventures in Wonderland" by Lewis Carroll is published.

1951 — "Alice in Wonderland" hits theaters.

1971 — Mad Tea Party is an Opening Day attraction in Magic Kingdom.

1974 — Florida is hot! The canopy is added to protect Mad Tea Party from the sun—& rain.

SPIN N' POINT!

In this game, one person spins the book while another player closes their eyes and tries to put their finger down on a spot on the page to score points. The first player to get **25+ points** wins.

The Story of Alice in Wonderland

Sitting with her sister and her cat Dinah on a riverbank, Alice sees the White Rabbit and is curious where he's headed. Following him, she falls down a hole into a strange place called Wonderland. She eats and drinks things that make her grow larger and smaller, and can't get a straight answer from any of the wacky characters she meets along the way—like Tweedle Dee, Tweedle Dum, a garden of talking flowers, the Caterpillar and the Cheshire Cat. After a crazy unbirthday party with the Mad Hatter, the March Hare and the Dormouse—who sleepily pops up out of a teapot—Alice decides she's ready to go home but gets lost in Tulgey Wood. The Cheshire Cat reappears and tells Alice to ask the Queen of Hearts how to get home. The hot-headed Queen orders "Off with her head!" and Alice runs away—with almost everyone from Wonderland chasing her—and wakes up back on the riverbank with her sister and Dinah. Was it all a dream?

DID YOU EAT IN FANTASYLAND?
☐ Yes ☐ No
If yes, where?
_____
What'd ya have?
_____
_____
_____

Was it good?
☐ Yes ☐ No
☐ Maybe So

FUN FACT
It's always winter at the Beast's castle. Through the windows of Be Our Guest, you can see snow gently falling outside.

PRETTY!

"If she doesn't eat with me, then she doesn't eat at all!"
—THE BEAST

★ Food & Drinks

Be Our Guest

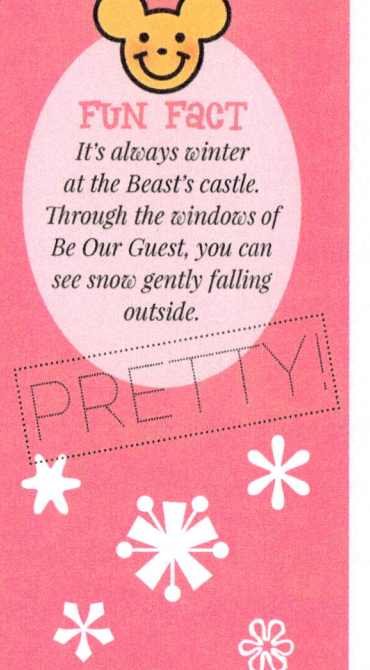

Walk across the stone bridge and through the grand entrance to enjoy a meal fit for royalty at this restaurant named for the famous song in *Beauty and the Beast*. You'll find gleaming chandeliers and a cherub-covered ceiling in the Grand Ballroom, elegant marble columns and tufted benches in the Castle Gallery, and deep purple walls and moody lighting in the West Wing. During dinner, you'll have a chance to visit with your host—the Beast!
• Eclairs • Eggs • French onion soup • Quiche • Steak

HOT TIP Be Our Guest's breakfast and lunch are **quick-service** but dinner is **full-service.**

SPY Look out for the **suits of armor** in the front hall and listen carefully to see if they're **saying anything!**

★ Meet n' Greets

Just down the path from Cheshire Café is Fairytale Garden where you can meet *Merida* from *Brave*, say hi to her bear brothers and brush up on your archery.

92

Cheshire Café

This cute quick-service café is sure to put a smile on your face. Named after the funny feline from Wonderland, this eatery has colorful umbrella-topped tables where you can enjoy your snack.
• Cheshire Cat tails • Coffee • Lemonade slushies

Cinderella's Royal Table

After a warm greeting from your hostess Cinderella, you'll take the red-carpeted stairs—or elevator—to the second floor of the castle. The regal dining room boasts soaring vaulted ceilings, colorful shields and banners, and stunning stained glass windows. As you dine, you'll enjoy visits from a variety of princesses and tasty delights from Cinderella's Royal Chef.
• Fish of the day • French toast • Salads • Soups

SPY: In the foyer at **Cinderella's Royal Table**, see if you can spot the little mice **Jaq and Gus** perched on a wall.

Gaston's Tavern

No one serves up yummy quick-service treats like Gaston! You can't miss the impressive fountain featuring Gaston and LeFou out front. Step inside this antler-filled restaurant to enjoy another tribute to your host hanging over the fireplace.
• Cinnamon buns • LeFou's Brew
• Stuffed pretzels • Veggies

SPY: Check the **score** on the **dartboard** to see who won the last match.

★ Meet n' Greets

You'll often find Gaston near his tavern showing off his dazzling wit—and muscles.

SO YOU KNOW... tavern = place for travelers to eat and drink

Pinocchio Village Haus

Step into the charming world of Pinocchio! Candy-colored stained glass windows and murals showing scenes from the puppet's adventures create a quaint setting for a quick-service, sit-down meal or snack.
• Chicken nuggets • Flatbreads • Pastas

HOT TIP Some tables here have a view of **Guests** boarding boats for **It's a Small World.**

★ That's Entertainment

Enjoy lessons in horse riding, proper manners and swordsmanship and other fun and games with **The Royal Majesty Makers** near the castle wall next to Pinocchio Village Haus or by the carousel.

The Story of Pinocchio

The woodcarver Geppetto makes a puppet named Pinocchio and wishes he were alive. The Blue Fairy uses her magic to make the wooden doll come to life but tells Pinocchio that he can never be a real boy until he is brave, truthful and unselfish. She asks Jiminy Cricket to be his conscience and help him to learn the difference between right and wrong. Pinocchio is supposed to go to school but lets Honest John the Fox and Gideon the Cat convince him to join the cast at Stromboli's puppet theater. Pinocchio becomes the star of the show but, when he wants to go home, Stromboli locks him up in a bird cage. The Blue Fairy comes to help but Pinocchio lies to her which makes his nose grow—and even sprout branches and leaves! When he promises to be good, the Blue Fairy fixes his nose and frees him. On his way home, he runs into Honest John and Gideon who convince him to go to Pleasure Island. Pinocchio makes friends with a boy named Lampwick and the two discover the island is cursed and turns children into donkeys. Luckily, Pinocchio escapes with only a donkey's ears and tail. When he gets home, he finds out Geppetto has gone to look for him and has been swallowed by Monstro the Whale. Pinocchio rushes off to bravely and unselfishly save Geppetto. The Blue Fairy decides that Pinocchio has proven himself worthy and turns him into a real boy.

"Now, let's eat before this crab wanders off my plate."
—GRIMSBY

Prince Eric's Village Market

Named after Ariel's favorite prince, this cute little tented stand is stacked with wooden crates filled with a variety of yummy grab-n-go snacks.
- Frozen lemonade • Fruits
- Hot pretzels • Veggies

Storybook Treats

Once upon a time there was a sweet, thatched cottage serving treats to enjoy on the go. And they all lived happily ever after. The end.
- Hot fudge sundaes • Soft-serve ice cream

The Friar's Nook

This handsome row of walk-up windows with hearty snacks is named after Friar Tuck, a badger in Disney's 1973 movie *Robin Hood* about a foxy outlaw who stole from the rich to give to the poor.
- Hot dogs • Lemonade slushies
- Mac n' cheese

Elena of Avalor!

★ Meet n' Greets

Next door to the Friar's Nook, you'll find Princess Fairytale Hall where you can meet Cinderella and Elena of Avalor or Rapunzel and Tiana.

Look near the castle wall next to Pinocchio Village Haus and you may find Cinderella characters like Anastasia, Drizella and the Fairy Godmother.

HEY KIDS COLOR ME IN!

★ Sample Souvenirs

"I've got something shiny for ya!"
—MOANA

CHARMING CHARMS

Here's a sweet souvenir that you can add to over time—a charm necklace or bracelet! Choose your chain style and which attachments you like best at **Sir Mickey's**, a vine-covered shop inspired by Disney's 1947 movie *Mickey and the Beanstalk*.

HOT TIP: This type of jewelry can also be found at several **other shops** around the resort.

EMBROIDERED EARS

Step right up to **Big Top Souvenirs** for the one, the only…mouse ear hat! First only made in basic black, these hats now come in a wide variety of colors and types, and many—but not all—can be custom-stitched with your name.

HOT TIP: In Magic Kingdom, only **Big Top Souvenirs**, **Le Chapeau** and **Curtain Call Collectibles** do personalized embroidery.

MAGICAL MAKEOVER

Fairy Godmothers-in-Training at **Bibbidi Bobbidi Boutique** are standing by here and in another location in Disney Springs. They'll work their magic with a variety of girly packages offering a choice of hairstyles, makeup, nail polish and more. The Knight Package offers young heroes a sword, shield and dashing, slicked-back hairstyle.

Disney Legend Close-Up: Dorothea Redmond

Dorthea Redmond was born in 1910. She went to Hollywood in 1938 to work in the movie business as the **first** female production designer, working on major movies like *Gone with the Wind* and *Rear Window*. In 1964 she became an **Imagineer** and went on to design interiors for restaurants and shops in Disneyland. When Magic Kingdom was being planned, Dorothea created gorgeous **concept art** for Main Street USA, Adventureland and Fantasyland, and designed the breathtaking **15-foot-tall murals** inside Cinderella Castle. Dorothea was named a Disney Legend in **2008**.

This Way, That Way, Yonder!

Search up and down Fantasyland to find these wondrous sights. Put a ✓ in the box next to the ones you find.

Fantasyland's charm is all in the details.

Tomorrowland

What Will You Find in This Chapter?

ATTRACTIONS
- Astro Orbiter
- Buzz Lightyear's Space Ranger Spin
- Carousel of Progress
- Monsters, Inc. Laugh Floor
- PeopleMover
- Space Mountain
- Tomorrowland Speedway

ENTERTAINMENT
- Dance Parties

FOOD & DRINKS
- Auntie Gravity's Galactic Goodies
- Cool Ship
- Cosmic Ray's Starlight Café
- Joffrey's Revive
- The Lunching Pad
- Tomorrowland Terrace

MEET N' GREETS
- Buzz Lightyear
- Stitch

ACTIVITIES, GAMES & INFO
- Racing Flags
- Make Your Own Cartoon!
- Be an Imagineer!
- Imagineers at Play
- Create a Knock Knock Joke!
- Sample Souvenirs
- Disney Legend Close-up: John Hench
- This Way, That Way, Yonder!

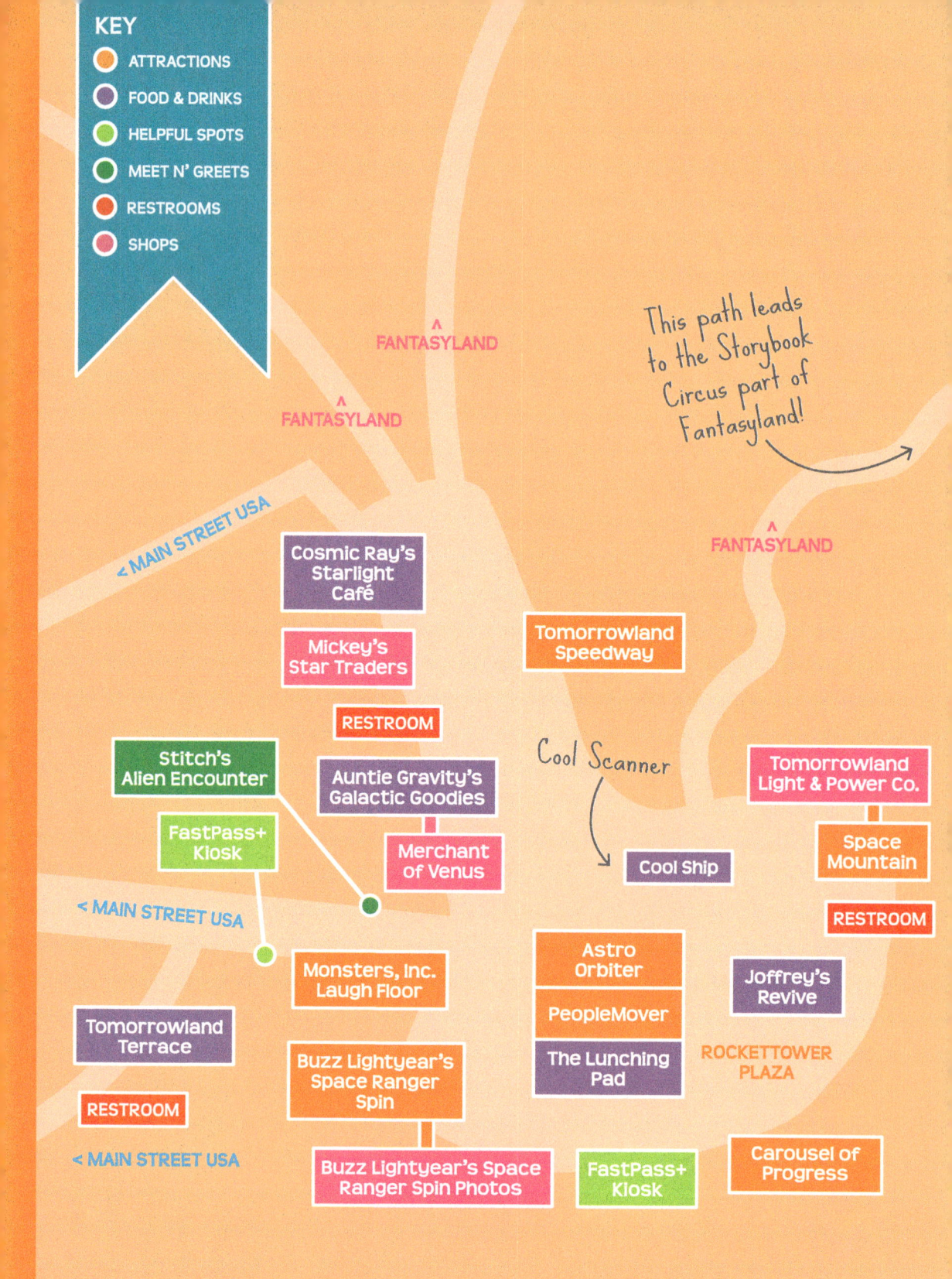

KEY

- 🟠 ATTRACTIONS
- 🟣 FOOD & DRINKS
- 🟢 HELPFUL SPOTS
- 🟩 MEET N' GREETS
- 🔴 RESTROOMS
- 🔺 SHOPS

^ FANTASYLAND

^ FANTASYLAND

This path leads to the Storybook Circus part of Fantasyland!

< MAIN STREET USA

^ FANTASYLAND

Cosmic Ray's Starlight Café

Mickey's Star Traders

Tomorrowland Speedway

RESTROOM

Cool Scanner

Stitch's Alien Encounter

Auntie Gravity's Galactic Goodies

Tomorrowland Light & Power Co.

FastPass+ Kiosk

Merchant of Venus

Cool Ship

Space Mountain

< MAIN STREET USA

RESTROOM

Monsters, Inc. Laugh Floor

Astro Orbiter

Joffrey's Revive

Tomorrowland Terrace

PeopleMover

RESTROOM

Buzz Lightyear's Space Ranger Spin

The Lunching Pad

ROCKETTOWER PLAZA

< MAIN STREET USA

Buzz Lightyear's Space Ranger Spin Photos

FastPass+ Kiosk

Carousel of Progress

MAP OF TOMORROWLAND

"I never look back, darling. It distracts from the now."
—EDNA MODE

A Better Tomorrow, Today

Travel back to the future in Tomorrowland! This land transports you to the furthest reaches of *outer space* with orbiting planets, rotating rockets and vibrant neon lights. A mixture of *retro* Space Age design and a modern tech vibe, this futuristic land is an *out of this world* place to enjoy attractions celebrating astronauts, intergalactic travel, aliens, monsters, cars, technology and even a *little bit* of history!

SO YOU KNOW...
Kugel = German word for sphere or ball

HOT TIP Check out the **Kugel ball** near Merchant of Venus. This is actually a globe with a map etched on it. Look for the **castle** representing Magic Kingdom!

Tomorrow **Land** **Space** **Rocket**

Waiting Game!

MAKE THE CONNECTION

The first player says a word—any word they like—and the next player says a word that's related to it. The words can be silly or not but it's especially fun if the players know each other well and can say words that are connected in a way only they would know. The play continues with each player saying a word related to the one said before it. Players continue, taking turns in order as long as they like.

RATE THIS ATTRACTION
- ☐ Never. Again.
- ☐ Not so hot.
- ☐ Pretty cool...
- ☐ Way cool!
- ☐ Awesome!!
- ☐ AHH, MY FAVE!!!

One word I'd use to describe this attraction:
_____

FUN FACT
When cars were first invented, they were steered with a lever. In 1894, a race car was fitted with a steering wheel & the rest is history.

NO WAY!

★ Tomorrowland Speedway

outdoor car ride — est. 1971 — lively & exciting

Get your motor running as you head out on the *Speedway!* Colorful flags flutter over the entrance to this car racing attraction. Hop behind the steering wheel and push *down* on the pedal to go and *release* it to slow down or stop. Winding around curves, you'll *zoom* past lush lawns and trees, and cruise under the PeopleMover tracks. Your journey ends at *Victory Circle* where you'll stop your car at the loading area and let the next driver take a spin!

HOT TIP: There's a **booth** at the ride's exit where you can buy a **driver's license**.

Which color car do you like best?
_____

Racing Flags

During a car race, **flagmen** wave colorful **flags** to communicate with **drivers**. So, what do these colors and patterns mean?

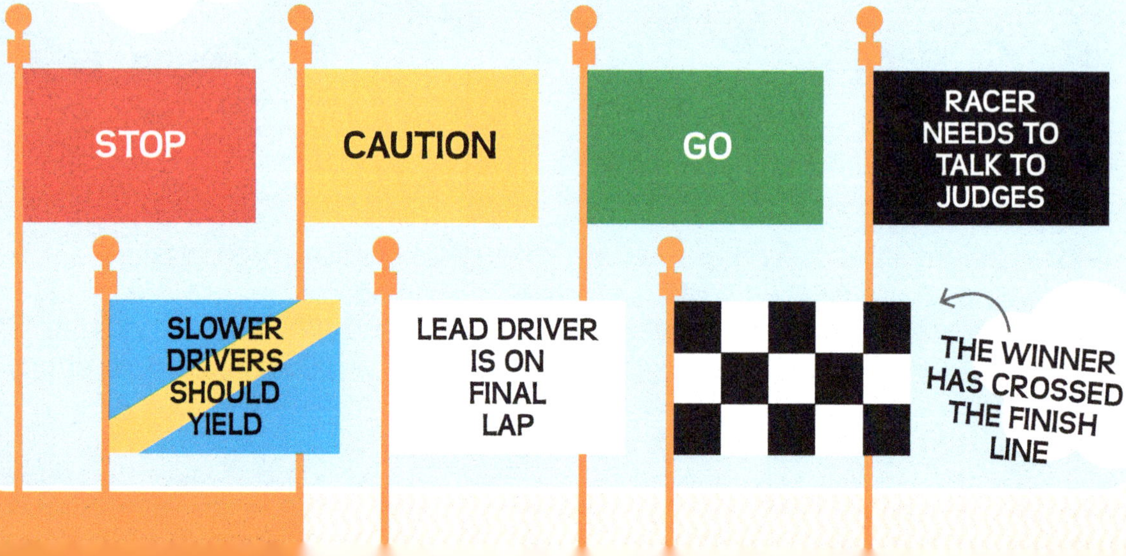

| STOP | CAUTION | GO | RACER NEEDS TO TALK TO JUDGES |

| SLOWER DRIVERS SHOULD YIELD | LEAD DRIVER IS ON FINAL LAP | (checkered) | THE WINNER HAS CROSSED THE FINISH LINE |

Make Your Own Cartoon!

Ready to star in your own comic? Draw a **three-panel comic strip** in each of the three rows below about **your adventures** on Tomorrowland Speedway—or **anywhere** in Magic Kingdom. Write the **title** above each strip and sign the **bottom right corner** of the last panel. Your main characters can be people, aliens, cars—anything goes, **YOU** are the artist.

TITLE: _____

TITLE: _____

TITLE: _____

RATE THIS ATTRACTION
- ☐ Never. Again.
- ☐ Not so hot.
- ☐ Pretty cool...
- ☐ Way cool!
- ☐ Awesome!!
- ☐ AHH, MY FAVE!!!

One word I'd use to describe this attraction:

_____

FUN FACT

Scientists think there may be "wormholes" in outer space—tunnels that would fold time & space to allow shortcuts on journeys across the universe.

TRIPPY!

★ Space Mountain

Roller Coaster — est. 1975 — Wild & Thrilling

MAY BE SCARY

Rocket through the universe on one of Magic Kingdom's most exciting *thrill rides* on a journey through deepest darkest space! You'll make your way through Starport 75 to a *launchpad* to board your rocket. When all systems are GO, you'll zoom into a tunnel *aglow* with pulsing lights towards a mysterious round, glowing orb. Once your rocket has *click-clacked* its way uphill, you'll dive and spiral past galaxies of comets, meteors and stars. *Blasting* through a wormhole, you'll suddenly find yourself back on Planet Earth, safe and sound!

SPY — Look for **coded signs** as you exit Space Mountain listing **Closed** and **Open Sectors**. The codes represent Magic Kingdom **lands and attractions**.

CLOSED SECTOR CODES

FL-20K	Fantasyland-20,000 Leagues Under the Sea: Submarine Voyage
FL-MTWR	Fantasyland-Mr. Toad's Wild Ride
TL-SK2FL	Tomorrowland-Skyway to Fantasyland
MSU-SB	Main Street USA-Swan Boats
FL-MMR	Fantasyland-Mickey Mouse Revue
TL-M2M	Tomorrowland-Mission to Mars

TIME MACHINE

1964 — Walt Disney approaches Imagineers with an idea for a roller coaster called Space Port or Space Voyage.

1960s — Imagineer John Hench sketches the iconic structure of Space Mountain.

1973 — Astronaut Gordon Cooper helps to design Space Mountain to make it as realistic as possible.

1975 — Blast off! Magic Kingdom gets its first thrill ride when Space Mountain opens.

104

Be an Imagineer!

What if you were one of the **Imagineers** who helped to create Space Mountain? Would you have made it **white**? Grab your **colored pencils** and create a new look for this famous ride.

HEY KIDS COLOR ME IN!

Imagineers at Play

Disney recently announced that one of the most popular rides in China's Shanghai Disneyland, **TRON Lightcycle Power Run,** will be added next to Space Mountain in Magic Kingdom. Based on Disney's 1982 *TRON* and 2010 *TRON: Legacy* movies, riders board a row of **Lightcycles** to enjoy a **roller coaster-type** thrill ride. The plan is for this attraction to open in time for Walt Disney World's **50th Anniversary** in 2021.

So, what do **you** think? Will you go on this new ride once it opens?
◼ Heck, yeah! ◼ Not sure… ◼ Not a chance!

RATE THIS ATTRACTION
- ☐ Never. Again.
- ☐ Not so hot.
- ☐ Pretty cool...
- ☐ Way cool!
- ☐ Awesome!!
- ☐ AHH, MY FAVE!!!

One word I'd use to describe this attraction:

_____

FUN FACT
A "gantry" is the structure that surrounds & supports a rocket before it takes off. Like Astro Orbiter, the gantry has an elevator so astronauts can reach the top of the rocket to climb in for their journey.

BLAST OFF!

MAY BE SCARY

★ Astro Orbiter

Pilot your own high-flying, **retro rocket** 'round and 'round the skies of Tomorrowland. Astro Orbiter is actually positioned about **60 feet** off the ground, on top of a raised platform that's reached by **elevator.** You'll board your rocket to orbit a towering structure that's encircled by a colorful solar system of **planets.** Once the ride begins, you'll control how low or high you fly by **pulling** and **pushing** a lever. Choose to hover near the base or reach for the stars!

Outdoor Spinning Ride • Lively & Exciting — est. 1974 —

HOT TIP: Be sure to try and ride at **night**! Because of the **height** of this ride, you'll have a **fabulous** view.

TIME MACHINE

1974 — Prepare for lift-off! Star Jets opens in Magic Kingdom.

1975 — Star Jets gets a new downstairs neighbor when WEDWay PeopleMover opens.

1994 — Star Jets reopen as Astro Orbiter & WEDWay PeopleMover's name changes to Tomorrowland Transit Authority.

2009 — PeopleMover is added back to the name, making it the Tomorrowland Transit Authority PeopleMover.

⭐ PeopleMover

Open-air Tram Ride · est. 1975 · calm & mellow

The full name of this ride is Tomorrowland Transit Authority PeopleMover. WHEW, that's awfully lo-o-o-ng, but you can just call it the *PeopleMover* like everyone else does! You'll go up a moving ramp to reach the *loading platform* where you'll step aboard. Once you're underway, your tram will transfer over to a slightly faster track—*whee!* Now it's time for you to sit back, relax and enjoy an outdoor and indoor tour of Tomorrowland. You'll even *pass through* the inside of Space Mountain and Buzz Lightyear's Space Ranger Spin. As you zip about, a *narrator* will explain where you are and what there is to see, including various displays and models. The PeopleMover, which creates *zero* pollution, does indeed *move people* but in the end you'll end up right back where you started.

SPY: Check out the model of Walt Disney's vision for the **Experimental Prototype Community of Tomorrow** inside one of PeopleMover's **tunnels.**

RATE THIS ATTRACTION
- ■ Never. Again.
- ■ Not so hot.
- ■ Pretty cool...
- ■ Way cool!
- ■ Awesome!!
- ■ AHH, MY FAVE!!!

One word I'd use to describe this attraction:
_____

FUN FACT
The area where you'll find Astro Orbiter, the PeopleMover entrance, & The Lunching Pad is named "Rockettower Plaza"—a play on the name of Rockefeller Plaza in New York City.

NEAT!

HOLDing on to the Magic

The PeopleMover also used to be a ride in Disneyland until it closed in 1995. In Magic Kingdom you can also still enjoy Carousel of Progress and Country Bear Jamboree—both of which have **closed** in Disneyland—and the **original** version of Swiss Family Treehouse which changed to Tarzan's Treehouse in Disneyland. Magic Kingdom attractions that you won't find in Disneyland resort—and were **never** there—include Enchanted Tales with Belle, Mickey's PhilharMagic, Seven Dwarfs Mine Train, The Barnstormer, The Hall of Presidents, The Magic Carpets of Aladdin and Monsters, Inc. Laugh Floor.

★ Carousel of Progress

RATE THIS ATTRACTION
- ☐ Never. Again.
- ☐ Not so hot.
- ☐ Pretty cool...
- ☐ Way cool!
- ☐ Awesome!!
- ☐ AHH, MY FAVE!!!

One word I'd use to describe this attraction:

_____

FUN FACT
The voice of the father in Carousel of Progress may sound familiar. Jean Shepherd also narrated (and wrote) the classic 1983 movie "A Christmas Story."

AH HA!

Take a seat in this truly *unique* rotating theater to get up to speed on the *progress* that's been made with inventions and innovations throughout recent history. Starting on Valentine's Day in the *1900s*, a friendly Audio-Animatronic father will tell you all about the handy-dandy new *gizmos* that are making life easier for him and his household. Jumping forward in time, you'll visit the family on Independence Day in the *1920s*, Halloween in the *1940s* and Christmastime in the *present* day. After each scene, the theater turns to reveal the next part of the stage as everyone joins together to sing, *There's a Great Big Beautiful Tomorrow.*

INDOOR SHOW ★ EST. 1975 ★ *Calm & Mellow*

SPY — It's easy to spot the family **dog** inside Carousel of Progress, but see if you can find their **cat**.

"Around here we don't look backwards for very long."
—WALT DISNEY

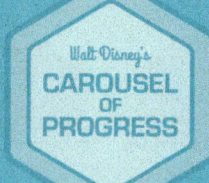

TIME MACHINE

1964
Beautiful! Carousel of Progress debuts at the New York World's Fair.

1967
Carousel of Progress opens in Disneyland where it delights Guests until closing in 1973.

1975
The attraction moves east & opens in Magic Kingdom.

1994
The attraction is officially renamed Walt Disney's Carousel of Progress because he originally created it.

Fun Facts about Carousel of Progress

The movie Father mentions starring Al Jolson is "The Jazz Singer." This movie changed history when it was released in 1927 with talking & singing that went along with the action, unlike the silent movies of the time.

The brothers from North Carolina that Father talks about are the Wright Brothers who invented & flew the first successful airplane in 1903.

"There's a Great Big Beautiful Tomorrow" is the original theme song for Carousel of Progress & was written by the Sherman Brothers. Richard & Robert Sherman also wrote songs you'll hear in It's a Small World & Enchanted Tiki Room.

Father marvels that buildings in the 1900s have gotten to be 20 stories tall. Today, the Willis Tower in Chicago, Illinois has 110 stories & the tallest buildings in the world have over 120 stories!

The voice of Uncle Orville & the pet parrot is none other than "The Man of a Thousand Voices," Mel Blanc. He was also the voice of Bugs Bunny & almost every other Looney Tunes cartoon character as well as Barney from "The Flintstones," Mr. Spacely from "The Jetsons" & Woody Woodpecker.

Carousel of Progress Mini Dictionary

Here's what some of the **words** and **phrases** you'll hear mean:

CANNING	Preserving food by sealing it in cans or jars
CISTERN	Reservoir or tank for holding water
CLODHOPPER	Clumsy goof
FUSE	Protects electrical circuits from harmful currents and and causes the power to go out when overloaded
HOOCHIE COOCHIE	Exotic dance like a belly dance
KEROSENE	Type of fuel used in lamps and heaters
LUMBAGO	Pain in the lower back
NINCOMPOOP	Old-fashioned word for a fool
PROGRESS	Growth or advancement
RUMP	Butt
RUMPUS ROOM	Play room or rec room

RATE THIS ATTRACTION
- ☐ Never. Again.
- ☐ Not so hot.
- ☐ Pretty cool...
- ☐ Way cool!
- ☐ Awesome!!
- ☐ AHH, MY FAVE!!!

One word I'd use to describe this attraction:

_____

FUN FACT
In "Toy Story 3," Buzz's BNL-brand batteries are from the Buy n' Large company seen in "WALL•E."

WOW!

★ Buzz Lightyear's Space Ranger Spin

Indoor Dark Ride — est. 1998 — Lively & Exciting

Take a spin through Buzz's world in this shooting gallery ride. Before you begin, Buzz will brief you on your mission—to stop evil **Emperor Zurg** and his army of robots from stealing batteries—or "crystallic fusion cells"—to power his new weapon. Next, it's time for Junior Space Rangers like you to report to your battle station, an **XP-37 Star Cruiser.** You'll use a joystick to spin into position and rack up points by zapping as many **"Z" targets** as you can with your laser cannon. At the end of the ride, check your score on the dashboard of your cruiser and compare it to the rankings on the **status board** on the wall. Will you be a **Star Cadet** or rule the galaxy as a **Galactic Hero?**

HOT TIP: If you **max out** your score with 999,999 points, take a **photo** and show it to a Cast Member for a free souvenir **certificate**.

★ Meet n' Greets

All systems are go to meet **Buzz Lightyear** next to his ride.

SCORING BIG ON BUZZ
- ★ Even if the ride stops, or you don't see anything to aim for, **never** stop firing
- ★ In the first room, the large robot's inner left arm target is worth **100,000 points**
- ★ Targets that are further away or moving are usually worth **more** points
- ★ When you find a good target, **fire again**—you get points each time you hit it

TIME MACHINE

1972 — If You Had Wings opens where Buzz's ride is now & changes its name to If You Could Fly in 1987.

1989 — Delta Dreamflight opens where If You Could Fly used to be & changes its name to Take Flight in 1998.

1995 — "Toy Story" hits theaters & is the first of many full-length & short movies featuring Buzz LIghtyear.

1998 — To infinity & beyond! Buzz Lightyear's Space Ranger Spin debuts in Magic Kingdom.

"Not today, Zurg!"
–BUZZ LIGHTYEAR

Buzz Lightyear, Sheriff Woody, Bo Peep, Etch, Hamm the Piggy Bank, Mr. and Mrs. Potato Head, Rex the Dinosaur, Slinky Dog and other toys belong to a boy named Andy and come to life when people aren't around. Woody is accidentally put out at a yard sale and is taken by the owner of Al's Toy Barn. Al plans to sell Woody and the other toys from the *Woody's Roundup* TV show—Jessie the Cowgirl, Bullseye the Horse and Stinky Pete the Prospector—to a museum in Japan. Buzz leads a group from Andy's room to rescue Woody and they end up at Al's Toy Barn where they have a run in with Emperor Zurg. This evil action figure comes from the same make-believe universe as Buzz and the Little Green Men aliens. Zurg thinks that Buzz is his enemy and tries to destroy him with his ion blaster. In the end, Woody, Jessie and Bullseye manage to escape from Al and make it to Andy's room with Buzz and the rest of the gang—and even three Little Green Men, who are adopted by Mr. and Mrs. Potato Head.

The Story of Toy Story 2

RATE THIS ATTRACTION
- ☐ Never. Again.
- ☐ Not so hot.
- ☐ Pretty cool...
- ☐ Way cool!
- ☐ Awesome!!
- ☐ AHH, MY FAVE!!!

One word I'd use to describe this attraction:

_____

★ Monsters, Inc. Laugh Floor

INDOOR SHOW — est. 2007 — Lively & exciting

Thank goodness the citizens of *Monstropolis* have figured out that laughs are better than screams! You'll go through a portal to Monstropolis and take a seat to enjoy *monstrously* funny jokes at the Laugh Floor comedy club. The more you laugh, the more *energy* will be collected in the giant yellow canister to the right of the stage. Your host is the wonderful Mike Wazowski, the club's *Monster of Ceremonies,* who'll introduce the various acts. Through it all, sarcastic Roz tunes in on a large screen to make sure the show is going well. The comedians include the *audience* in their act so don't be surprised if you suddenly see yourself *or* someone sitting near you caught on camera!

FUN FACT
The sushi restaurant in "Monsters, Inc." is called Harryhausen's as a tribute to famous special effects artist Ray Harryhausen who made stop-motion monster movies with small, moveable models.

RAD!

HOT TIP: While waiting to go in to the Laugh Floor, you'll find out how to **text a joke** to the comedians. Mike's nephew **Marty Wazowski** will tell some of the Guests' jokes during the show!

TIME MACHINE

1971 — Circle-Vision 360 Theater opens & hosts shows like American Journeys, Magic Carpet 'Round the World & The Timekeeper.

2001 — We scare because we care! The world meets Mike & Sulley when "Monsters, Inc." hits theaters.

2007 — Monsters, Inc. Laugh Floor debuts in Magic Kingdom where Circle-Vision 360 Theater used to be.

2013 — "Monsters University," about Mike & Sulley's college days, hits theaters.

Create a Knock Knock Joke!

Fill in a funny ending for the jokes below. The first one's been done for you.

Knock knock!
Who's there?
Boo
Boo who?
Aw, don't cry... you'll be okay!

Knock knock!
Who's there?
Ice Cream
Ice cream who?
Ice cream every time I see...

Knock knock!
Who's there?
Mikey
Mikey who?
Mikey won't work, please...

Knock knock!
Who's there?
Celia
Celia who?
Celia later, I've gotta go...

Knock knock!
Who's there?
Roz
Roz who?
Roz and shine, it's time to...

The Story of Monsters, Inc.

The city of Monstropolis runs on the power from the screams of terrified children. Because the monsters think human kids are full of dangerous germs, the city is policed by the CDA, or Child Detection Agency. Big, scary monster James P. Sullivan (nicknamed "Sulley") and his best friend and assistant, one-eyed Mike Wazowski work together at Monsters, Inc. to go through kids' closet doors to scare them and collect their scream energy. Through it all, supervisor Roz is "always watching." After a human girl they call Boo follows Sulley into the monsters' world, Mike and Sulley realize the power of her laughter is much more powerful than her screams. A chameleon-like co-worker named Randall tries to ruin their plans but Mike and Sully get Boo back home, safe and sound. Now, instead of going into children's rooms to scare them, the monsters make them laugh—something that comes naturally to funny Mike and his new assistant Sulley.

| DID YOU EAT IN TOMORROWLAND? |
| ☐ Yes ☐ No |
| If yes, where? |
| _____ |
| What'd ya have? |
| _____ |
| _____ |
| _____ |
| Was it good? |
| ☐ Yes ☐ No |
| ☐ Maybe So |

FUN FACT
On Opening Day, Tomorrowland had just two attractions: Skyway to Fantasyland (which is no longer) & Grand Prix Raceway, which is now called Tomorrowland Speedway.

WHOA!

★ Food & Drinks ★

Auntie Gravity's Galactic Goodies

A play on the term "anti-gravity," this quick-service spot is the place for yummy frozen treats.
• Ice cream sundaes • Smoothies • Soft-serve ice cream

Cool Ship

What's cooler than cool? Grabbing a bite at a futuristic snack stand connected to a spaceship-shaped water mister!
• Pizza
• Soda

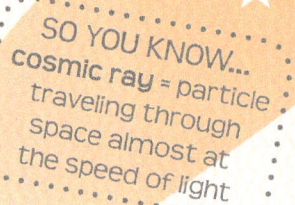

SO YOU KNOW... **cosmic ray** = particle traveling through space almost at the speed of light

Cosmic Ray's Starlight Café

Here you'll find hearty meals that can be customized at a stellar toppings bar. This colorful café has three separate ordering bays—one for chicken, one for burgers and one for salads.
• Burgers with fries • Chicken nuggets
• Rotisserie chicken • Sandwiches

HOT TIP Find a seat near the stage to enjoy alien **Sonny Eclipse** performing on an astro-organ while you eat.

114

"No more caffeine for you."
—Lilo

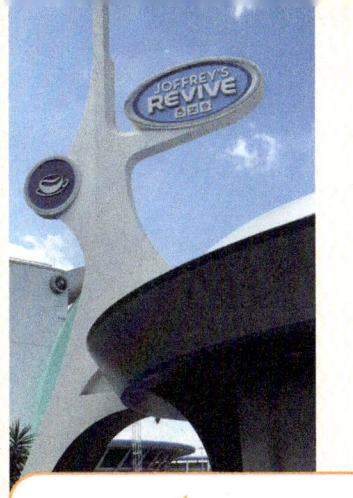

Joffrey's Revive

The cool retro-futuristic shape of the sign for this walk-up stand pays tribute to one of Tomorrowland's past attractions—Mission to Mars. Land here for hot or cold coffee, tea and more.
• Coffee • Pastries • Tea

The Lunching Pad

Named after a "launching pad" where rockets take off into outer space, these walk-up windows are located under the rockets of Astro Orbiter.
• Frozen slushies • Hot dogs
• Stuffed pretzels

★ That's Entertainment

See if Rockettower Plaza next to Joffrey's Revive is hosting any **Dance Parties** during your visit!

SPY See if your call can get through on the **Metrophone** next to The Lunching Pad.

Tomorrowland Terrace

This quick-service spot features a futuristic patio with lovely views. None of the tables here are indoors but ceiling fans, covered seating and breezes off the nearby water make this a cool place to catch a meal.
• Cheeseburgers • Chicken strips • Salads • Sandwiches

HOT TIP **Tomorrowland Terrace** boasts awesome views of the **fireworks** over Cinderella Castle. For an **extra fee**, you can reserve a great viewing spot for the restaurant's **dessert parties**.

★ Meet n' Greets

Enjoy a visit with *Stitch* at Stitch's Alien Encounter just down the path from The Lunching Pad.

Imagineers at Play

Recently, a theater-in-the-round attraction called **Stitch's Great Escape** changed to a Meet n' Greet called **Stitch's Alien Encounter**. Perhaps the attraction will reopen someday or perhaps Imagineers are going to create something new.

So, what do **you** think? What would you rather see here?
■ Stitch's Alien Encounter!   ■ Stitch's Great Escape!   ■ Something new!

Sample Souvenirs

"Your eyes can deceive you. Don't trust them."
—OBI-WAN KENOBI

Fun Photos

Imagining yourself as your favorite character is easy at **Merchant of Venus.** Choose which image you'd like and a Cast Member will take your photo and add you to it. The new picture can then be turned into a photo print, poster, key chain or even a velveteen blanket! This shop's name is a nod to *The Merchant of Venice,* a play by William Shakespeare.

Tricked-Out Phone

Protect your phone with a custom-printed case at **Tomorrowland Light & Power Co.** Choose the size, side color and art style, and whether you want your name on it or not. The case prints out in minutes, ready for you to pop it on your phone!

HOT TIP: Tomorrowland Light & Power Co. also offers **custom-printed MagicBands.**

SPY: Look in this shop for a **trivia quiz** on an erasable whiteboard. See how many questions **you** can get right!

Disney Legend Close-Up: John Hench

John Hench was born in Iowa in **1908** and went to art school in New York City and Los Angeles before eventually becoming "the guru of Disney design." He started in 1939 in the **animation department** where he helped out on *Fantasia, Dumbo* and *Cinderella* to name a few. After creating **special effects** for *20,000 Leagues Under the Sea,* John began his Imagineering career. You can thank John for **two** of the most famous structures in any Disney park—**Space Mountain** and **Cinderella Castle.** One of the lessons John learned from **Walt Disney** was to go to the parks and walk around like a regular Guest. After those visits, he'd always have lots of **notes** on how to make things **even better.** During his long career, John was also the **official portrait artist** for Mickey Mouse. At 95 years old, he was still working full-time for Disney when he passed away. John was named a Disney Legend in **1990.**

This Way, That Way, Yonder!

Search up and down **Tomorrowland** to find these stellar sights. Put a ✓ in the box next to the ones you find.

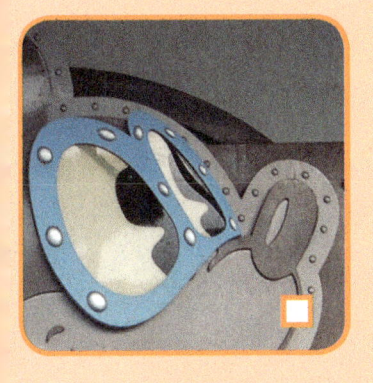

Gear up for futuristic shopping in Tomorrowland Light & Power Co.

Liberty Square

What Will You Find in This Chapter?

ATTRACTIONS
- Haunted Mansion
- Liberty Square Riverboat
- The Hall of Presidents

ENTERTAINMENT
- The Muppets Present Great Moments in American History

FOOD & DRINKS
- Columbia Harbour House
- Liberty Square Market
- Liberty Tree Tavern
- Sleepy Hollow
- The Diamond Horseshoe

MEET N' GREETS
- *Mary Poppins* Characters

ACTIVITIES, GAMES & INFO
- The Muppets Primer
- Disney Legend Close-up: Wathel Rogers
- Say What? Villains Edition!
- Sample Souvenirs
- This Way, That Way, Yonder!

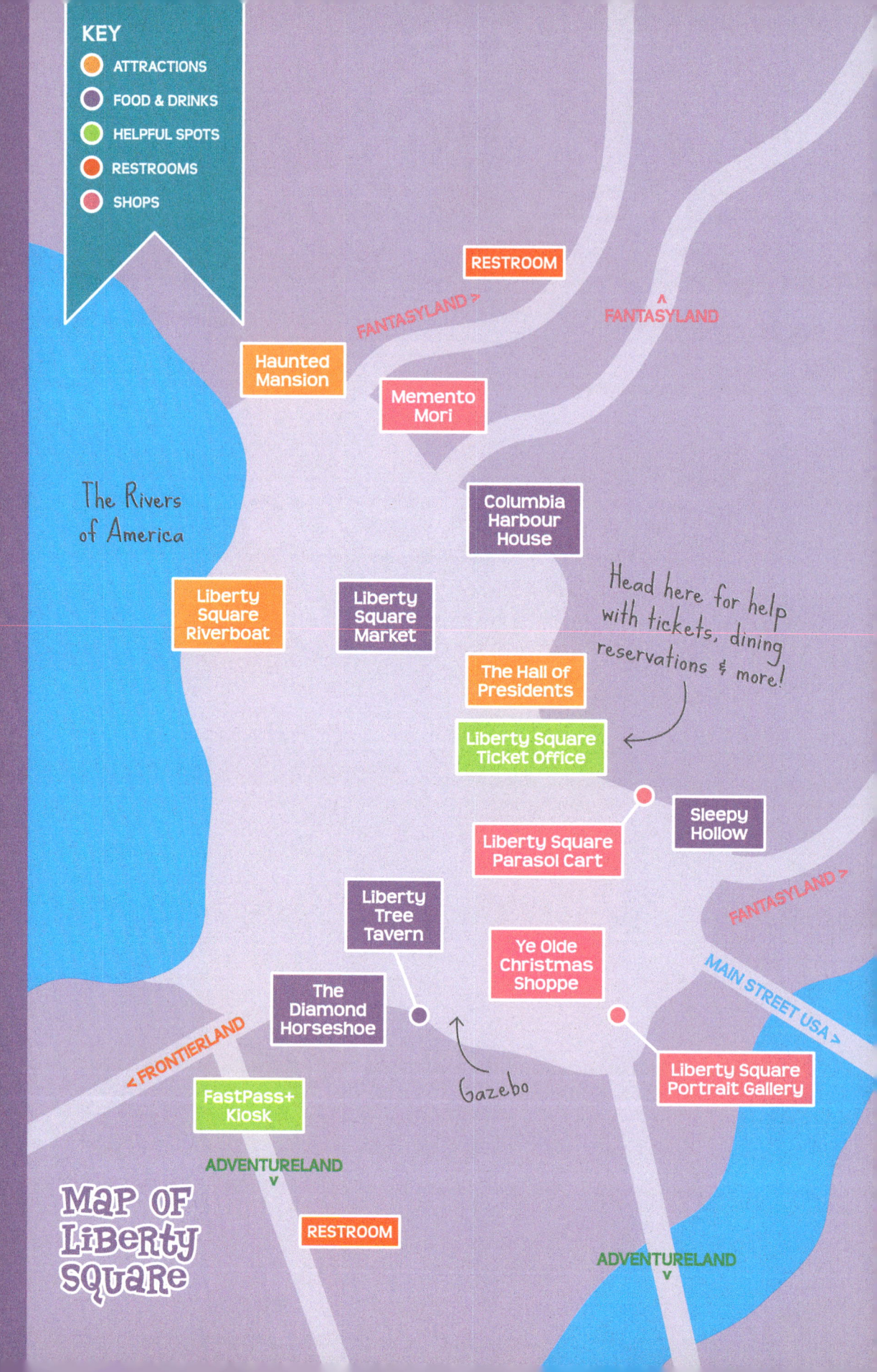

Map of Liberty Square

KEY
- 🟠 ATTRACTIONS
- 🟣 FOOD & DRINKS
- 🟢 HELPFUL SPOTS
- 🔴 RESTROOMS
- 🩷 SHOPS

- RESTROOM
- FANTASYLAND >
- ^ FANTASYLAND
- Haunted Mansion
- Memento Mori
- The Rivers of America
- Columbia Harbour House
- Liberty Square Riverboat
- Liberty Square Market
- *Head here for help with tickets, dining reservations & more!*
- The Hall of Presidents
- Liberty Square Ticket Office
- Liberty Square Parasol Cart
- Sleepy Hollow
- Liberty Tree Tavern
- Ye Olde Christmas Shoppe
- FANTASYLAND >
- The Diamond Horseshoe
- Gazebo
- MAIN STREET USA >
- < FRONTIERLAND
- Liberty Square Portrait Gallery
- FastPass+ Kiosk
- ADVENTURELAND v
- RESTROOM
- ADVENTURELAND v

> "And in the end, it's not the years in your life that count. It's the life in your years."
> —ABRAHAM LINCOLN

Give Me Liberty

SO YOU KNOW...
colonists = people from a different country who have settled in a new country

Step back in time to America's *early days* in Liberty Square! Quaint wooden shutters, brick buildings and hitching posts for horses *recreate* the time when **colonists** declared their independence from England and formed a brand new country called—you guessed it—the United States of America. In the center of the square stands the *Liberty Tree* strung with thirteen lanterns— one for each of the original states.

SPY: Look near Liberty Square Market for the **pillory** and **stocks.** A pillory holds a person's **hands** and **head** in place and stocks hold their **hands** and **feet.** These devices were used in the old days on naughty people to punish them in front of their fellow townspeople.

WHAT COLOR IS tHE BENCH WE'RE SITTING ON?

Waiting Game!

LOOK/DON'T LOOK
This game is to be played with two players when they're sitting in one spot. After both people have carefully looked at their surroundings, one player closes their eyes and the other asks a detailed question about something around them. As soon as the first player answers they may open their eyes to see if they were right and the second player must close their eyes and wait for the other player to ask them a question. Players continue, taking turns in order as long as they like.

★ The Hall of Presidents

How would you like to hang out with every single U.S. President there ever was? This Audio-Animatronic show featuring American leaders from George Washington onward is about as close as you can get! First, you'll step into an elegant **rotunda** where you can check out Presidential artifacts. Once you enter the theater and take a seat, you'll view two short movies about America's rich history and hear a few words from Abraham Lincoln. The curtain will rise to reveal the entire group of Presidents who'll be introduced in the order they served the country.

SPY: The Hall of Presidents had to get special permission to use the **Great Seal of the United States.** Look for it on the **carpet** in the rotunda.

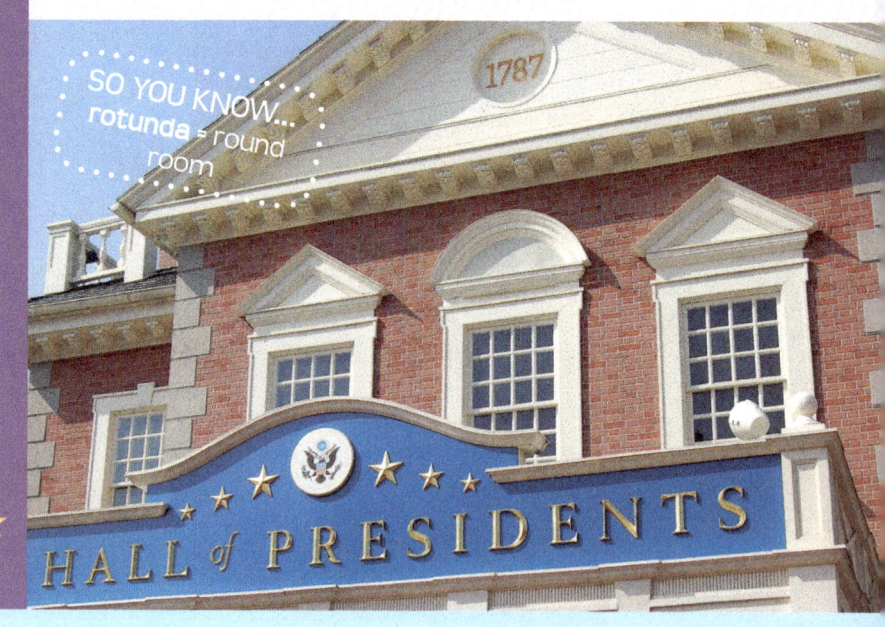

INDOOR SHOW — est. 1971 — CALM & MELLOW

RATE THIS ATTRACTION
- ☐ Never. Again.
- ☐ Not so hot.
- ☐ Pretty cool...
- ☐ Way cool!
- ☐ Awesome!!
- ☐ AHH, MY FAVE!!!

One word I'd use to describe this attraction:
_____

FUN FACT
The window of The Hall of Presidents' building that faces the Rivers of America has two lanterns in it. This represents the signal that Americans used to warn each other about British forces approaching—"One if by land, two if by sea."

SO YOU KNOW... rotunda = round room

TIME MACHINE

1787 — The U.S. Constitution is signed in Independence Hall—which The Hall of Presidents' building is designed to look like.

1789 — I cannot tell a lie, George Washington becomes America's first President.

1971 — The Hall of Presidents is an Opening Day attraction in Magic Kingdom.

1993 — Bill Clinton is the first President to have his voice recorded to be used in the attraction.

The Muppets Primer

NAME
Fozzie Bear
QUOTE
"Wocka! Wocka!"
KNOWN FOR
Telling corny jokes

NAME
Gonzo the Great
QUOTE
"Put me down as a…whatever."
KNOWN FOR
Having a great fondness for chickens

NAME
Kermit the Frog
QUOTE
"With good friends you can't lose."
KNOWN FOR
Being the boss

NAME
Miss Piggy
QUOTE
"Who better to play royalty than moi?"
KNOWN FOR
Loving herself and Kermit

NAME
Sam Eagle
QUOTE
"Is nothing sacred?"
KNOWN FOR
Being patriotic, *very* patriotic

★ That's Entertainment

The Muppets make history fun with jokes, stories and songs! Gather 'round the front of The Hall of Presidents as *The Muppets Present Great Moments in American History* in different shows throughout the day—sometimes with the help of town crier James Jefferson.

Disney Legend Close-Up: Wathel Rogers

Wathel Rogers was born in 1919 in Colorado and grew up constructing **toys** from objects he'd find around the house. After art school in Los Angeles, he began working as a **Disney animator**, working on classics like *Pinocchio, Cinderella, Alice in Wonderland, Peter Pan* and *Lady and the Tramp*. Because of his natural **sculpting** and **building** talents, Wathel began creating props and miniatures for live-action movies and television shows. In 1954, Walt Disney asked Wathel to help create models for Disneyland—the start of his career in the **Imagineering** department. Wathel, who became known as "Mr. Audio-Animatronics," worked on **Carousel of Progress** and the **Abraham Lincoln** figure for the 1964 New York World's Fair. He also helped out with Enchanted Tiki Room, Jungle Cruise and **Haunted Mansion** and was the **first field art director** for Walt Disney World. Wathel was named a Disney Legend in **1995**.

★ Haunted Mansion

MAY BE SCARY

RATE THIS ATTRACTION
- ■ Never. Again.
- ■ Not so hot.
- ■ Pretty cool...
- ■ Way cool!
- ■ Awesome!!
- ■ AHH, MY FAVE!!!

One word I'd use to describe this attraction:
_____

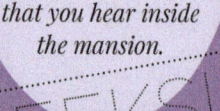

INDOOR DARK RIDE — EST. 1971 — LIVELY & EXCITING

Welcome, foolish mortals! Step inside this home of **999 happy haunts** to enter an eight-sided chamber. You'll hear the **disembodied** voice of your Ghost Host as eerie portraits stretch right before your eyes. Once you find your way out, you'll climb aboard a **Doom Buggy** and pass peculiar paintings to travel through a library filled with dusty books and curious statues. Winding through the dark mansion, a **mysterious** piano plays itself and a wretched creature cries to you from inside a **creaking** coffin. Hallways lined with **demon eye** wallpaper and rows of sinister doors lead to the seance room where the floating head of **Madame Leota** summons the spirits to appear. Next, it's on to the ballroom where ghosts have gathered to dance, dine and duel. Moving through the attic, you'll hear the thumping heartbeat of the wicked bride Constance Hatchaway as she pledges her **undying** devotion to a **string** of unlucky husbands. In the end, a graveyard is alive with gleeful ghosts but—**beware**—one of them might just try to follow you home!

FUN FACT
Some of Haunted Mansion's tombstones honor Imagineers like Francis Xavier Atencio who wrote the song "Grim Grinning Ghosts" that you hear inside the mansion.

EEKS!

HOT TIP: Pay close attention and you just may hear the **gargoyle candelabras** in the stretching room **whispering.**

SPY: Look up to spy **Little Leota** with a final message for you. She's just **dying** to have you hurry **ba-ack.**

TIME MACHINE

1971 — Haunted Mansion is an Opening Day attraction in Magic Kingdom.

2005 — A six-part comic series begins featuring Master Gracey, the owner of the mansion whose portrait is in the foyer.

2007 — The ghosts do a bit of remodeling including adding a strange staircase with glowing footprints. Boo-tiful!

2011 — Interactive fun is added to the regular standby line for Haunted Mansion.

"I do. I did."
—CONSTANCE

125

Say What? Villains Edition!

Guess **which** villain said **what**. Draw a **line** connecting their name with the quote. The first one's been done for you. *Answers on page 191.*

Whoa—is my hair out?

This is just a minor setback in a major operation!

I say we kill the Beast!

Dr. Facilier
The Princess and the Frog, 2009

Gaston
Beauty and the Beast, 1991

How many times do I have to kill you, boy?

You poor, simple fools, thinking you could defeat me! ME! The mistress of all evil!

Hades
Hercules, 1997

Jafar
Aladdin, 1992

Lady Tremaine
Cinderella, 1950

There's the large carpet in the main hall—clean it!

Maleficent
Sleeping Beauty, 1959

Mother Gothel
Tangled, 2010

And when you are growing too old, you will make good firewood!

Stromboli
Pinocchio, 1940

The Evil Queen
Snow White and the Seven Dwarfs, 1937

You are not leaving this tower. EVER!

Ursula
The Little Mermaid, 1989

Life's full of tough choices, isn't it?

But to make doubly sure you do not fail, bring back her heart in this.

⭐ Liberty Square Riverboat

Outdoor Boat Ride • Calm & Mellow • EST. 1971

Tour the Rivers of America aboard the *beautiful* Liberty Belle! This working replica of a 19th-century steam-powered paddle wheeler departs from *Liberty Square* and makes a loop around Tom Sawyer Island. As you enjoy your ride, listen up for messages from the Captain about the interesting *sights to see*. During your journey, you can find a seat and *relax* or explore the boat to check out the Main Deck, the Promenade Deck, the Texas Deck and the *Pilothouse*, where the Captain's Quarters and Wheelhouse are located.

HOT TIP: For an extra fee, you can enjoy an **ice cream social** on the dock with **Princess Tiana** and **Prince Naveen** from *The Princess and the Frog* and watch a parade from the riverboat.

RATE THIS ATTRACTION
- ☐ Never. Again.
- ☐ Not so hot.
- ☐ Pretty cool...
- ☐ Way cool!
- ☐ Awesome!!
- ☐ AHH, MY FAVE!!!

One word I'd use to describe this attraction:
_____

FUN FACT
Technically, Liberty Square Riverboat is not an Opening Day attraction but it was ready for riders on the second day the park was open.

SUPER!

What was your favorite thing you saw from the deck of the Liberty Belle?
_____
_____

DID YOU EAT IN LIBERTY SQUARE?
☐ Yes ☐ No
If yes, where?
_____
_____

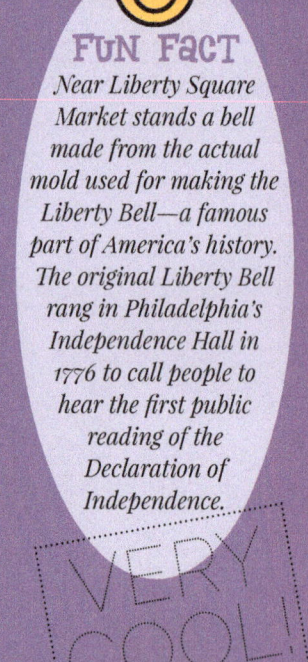

What'd ya have?
_____
_____
_____

Was it good?
☐ Yes ☐ No
☐ Maybe So

FUN FACT
Near Liberty Square Market stands a bell made from the actual mold used for making the Liberty Bell—a famous part of America's history. The original Liberty Bell rang in Philadelphia's Independence Hall in 1776 to call people to hear the first public reading of the Declaration of Independence.

VERY COOL!

"Part of the secret of success in life is to eat what you like and let the food fight it out inside."
—MARK TWAIN

COLUMBIA HARBOUR HOUSE
CHICKEN SANDWICHES SEAFOOD

★ Food & Drinks

Columbia Harbour House

Ahoy there! This large, quick-service eatery is named for the Columbia Rediviva, the first American ship to circle the globe. Wood trim and paneling, braided ship's ropes and nautical steering wheels decorate the cozy dining rooms.
• Clam chowder • Fried fish • Lobster rolls • Salads

SPY: See how many **figureheads** you can spot inside Columbia Harbour House. These **wooden carvings** are used to decorate the fronts of ships.

Liberty Square Market

Hear ye, hear ye! Here ye can find a colonial-style pavilion with wagons and barrels filled with healthy fruits, veggies and other snacks to enjoy on the go.
• Hot dogs • Pickles
• Trail mix • Turkey legs

Liberty Tree Tavern

It's easy to imagine it's the 1700s when you step inside this quaint tavern. Cast Members dressed in early American clothing provide full-service dining in an old-fashioned setting with rustic stone walls, brick fireplaces and candlelit chandeliers. Tuck in to an all-you-care-to-enjoy feast for one fixed price.
• *Pot roast* • *Pasta with shrimp* • *Roasted turkey breast*

HOT TIP: You can order **individual items** from the menu during lunch only.

Sleepy Hollow

Washington Irving's *The Legend of Sleepy Hollow* about Ichabod Crane, Katrina Van Tassel and the town of Sleepy Hollow being terrorized by the Headless Horseman was published in 1820 and was part of Disney's *The Adventures of Ichabod and Mr. Toad* movie from 1949. Stop by the walk-up windows at this quick-service brick cottage for legendary sweet treats and snacks—and a fab view of Cindy's castle across the way!
• *Baked potatoes* • *Funnel cakes* • *Pretzel dogs*
• *Waffle sandwiches*

The Diamond Horseshoe

This full-service saloon serves down-home fare in a Western setting. Just be sure you're mighty hungry because the vittles here are served up all-you-care-to-enjoy style.
• *Barbecued meats* • *Brownies* • *Salads*

Katrina!

HEY KIDS COLOR ME IN!

★ Meet n' Greets

See if Mary Poppins characters have popped by the gazebo behind Liberty Tree Tavern.

"What we want, what we need...all the same thing, yes?"
—PRINCE NAVEEN

⭐ Sample Souvenirs

Custom Xmas Ornament

It's Christmas every day at **Ye Olde Christmas Shoppe!** This shop has all sorts of holiday goodies and a terrific selection of ornaments, many of which can be hand painted for an extra fee by in-store artists with your name, a special date or a meaningful message.

HOT TIP: The artists in **Ye Old Christmas Shoppe** are happy to personalize other souvenirs from **other shops** around the park too.

SPY: Look **outside** Ye Olde Christmas Shoppe for a **sign** that says **Kepple**—Walt and Roy's grandfather's name.

Paper Silhouette

Amazingly skilled paper artists cut your **silhouette** freehand in about 60 seconds at two outdoor carts in Magic Kingdom —one in **Liberty Square Portrait Gallery** and the other in Main Street USA.

SO YOU KNOW... silhouette = solid black shape made from the outline of an object

HOT TIP: Your **favorite Disney character** can also be ordered—or added to your portrait!

Pretty Parasol

The **Liberty Square Parasol Cart** offers ruffled umbrellas for rain or shine that can be customized with lettering, characters, hearts, flowers and more. Choose your parasol size and color and the artist will hand-paint a special design just for you.

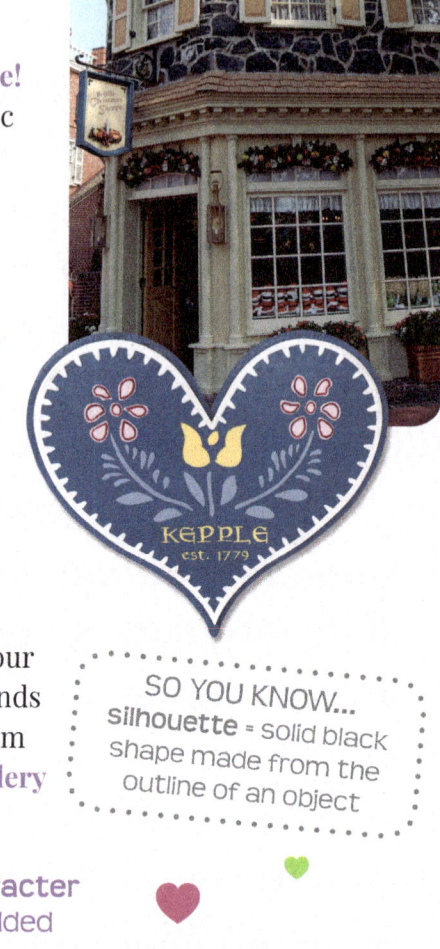

Spirit Photography

Step inside the photo booth in **Memento Mori** to let the spirits capture your image in a spooky portrait that changes your face from normal to ghoulishly grim as you move the portrait back and forth.

This Way, That Way, Yonder!

Search up and down **Liberty Square** to find these interesting sights. Put a ✓ in the box next to the ones you find.

Haunted Mansion's roof features every chess piece except the Knight because it's always night inside the mansion.

Adventureland

What Will You Find in This Chapter?

ATTRACTIONS
- Enchanted Tiki Room
- Jungle Cruise
- Pirates of the Caribbean
- Swiss Family Treehouse
- The Magic Carpets of Aladdin

ENTERTAINMENT
- Captain Jack Sparrow's Pirate Tutorial

FOOD & DRINKS
- Aloha Isle
- Skipper Canteen
- Sunshine Tree Terrace
- Tortuga Tavern

MEET N' GREETS
- *Aladdin* Characters

ACTIVITIES, GAMES & INFO
- Animal Hunt!
- A Pirate's Life for You
- Orange You a Cute Little Bird
- Sample Souvenirs
- Disney Legend Close-up: Harriet Burns
- This Way, That Way, Yonder!

MAP OF ADVENTURELAND

KEY
- ATTRACTIONS
- FOOD & DRINKS
- HELPFUL SPOTS
- RESTROOMS
- SHOPS

< FRONTIERLAND
< LIBERTY SQUARE
MAIN STREET USA >

- FastPass+ Kiosk
- Agrabah Bazaar
- Zanzibar Trading Co.
- Island Supply
- RESTROOM
- Skipper Canteen
- Aloha Isle
- ARABIAN VILLAGE
- Enchanted Tiki Room
- The Magic Carpets of Aladdin
- Sunshine Tree Terrace
- Tortuga Tavern
- Outdoor Stage
- Leaky Tikis
- Swiss Family Treehouse
- The Crow's Nest
- CARIBBEAN PLAZA
- FastPass+ Kiosk
- Bwana Bob's
- La Princesa de Cristal
- Jungle Cruise
- RESTROOM
- Pirates of the Caribbean
- The Pirates League
- Plaza del Sol Caribe Bazaar

Name inspired by Bob Hope in the movie "Call Me Bwana" from 1963!

> "Such a thing would be greater than all the magic and all the treasures in all the world!"
> —GENIE

Here Is Adventure

Travel to the furthest reaches of the *globe* in Adventureland! Elements of African, Asian, Caribbean, Middle Eastern, Polynesian and South American cultures *blend* in this land dotted with exotic flowers and tropical palms. Stroll past brightly colored buildings draped with silken *canopies* in an Arabian village. Nearby, a mysterious *pagoda* towers over the tile rooftops of the sun-bleached Caribbean Plaza.

SPY: Be sure to notice the colorful **masks**, carved **tikis** and stacked **skulls** on the awesome sign for Adventureland.

There once was a lonely pirate on a deserted island.

His best friends were a coconut and a shell.

One day...

Waiting Game!

TRUE-LIFE ADVENTURES

In 1948, Disney began making documentary films called *True-Life Adventures* that later went on to be an inspiration for Jungle Cruise. In this game, players tell an adventure story together by creating one sentence at a time in turn. Anything goes and players can get imaginative—the sillier the better. Players continue, taking turns in order as long as they like. When one of the players feels like the story has run its course they can wrap it up and say, "The End."

RATE THIS ATTRACTION
- ☐ Never. Again.
- ☐ Not so hot.
- ☐ Pretty cool...
- ☐ Way cool!
- ☐ Awesome!!
- ☐ AHH, MY FAVE!!!

One word I'd use to describe this attraction:
_____

FUN FACT
The treehouse is in a special type of banyan tree dubbed the *Disneyodendron eximus*, which stands about 60 ft. tall & 90 ft. wide with over 300,000 leaves.

WHEW!

★ Swiss Family Treehouse

OUTDOOR WALK-THROUGH · EST. 1971 · CALM & MELLOW

Wind your way through the tale of the **Robinson** family! See firsthand what treehouse living is like when you walk—**and climb**—at your own pace through the family's island home. You'll see clever **innovations** that make life easier—like a bamboo wheel that carries water up into the tree and a sink made from a giant **clamshell**. Peek into the living room, sleeping quarters, library and kitchen as you make your way up to the **tippity top** of the tree and back down again.

HOT TIP: Be ready for some **exercise!** To get to the **topmost point** you'll have to walk up over **100 stairs**. But, what a view!

SPY: Listen up for a **merry tune** playing on the Robinson family's **organ**—it's the Swisskapolka!

TIME MACHINE

1812 — The book "Swiss Family Robinson" by Johann David Wyss is published.

1960 — All the thrills...all the laughter...all the excitement! "Swiss Family Robinson" hits theaters.

1971 — Swiss Family Treehouse is an Opening Day attraction in Magic Kingdom.

2016 — The bamboo throne & colorful flags from New Switzerland's holiday festivities are added to the treehouse.

136

"Everything we need—everything—right here, right at our fingertips."
—FATHER ROBINSON

The Story of Swiss Family Robinson

Father and Mother Robinson and their sons Fritz, Ernst and Francis are traveling by ship from Switzerland to New Guinea in the 1800s when they are shipwrecked onto a deserted island. As they are saving items from the ship, pirates attack but the family manages to scare them away. Father, Fritz and Ernst build an amazing treehouse for the family to live in. While exploring the island, Fritz and Ernst discover that the pirates have captured another ship and taken two prisoners—the ship's Captain and his grandson Bertie. The boys rescue Bertie and discover he's actually a girl named Roberta. Back at the treehouse, Father, Mother and Francis welcome Roberta to their home and everyone dances while Mother plays the Swisskapolka on the organ. Later, when Fritz and Ernst fight over Roberta, Father distracts them by declaring that the next day will be the first holiday for "New Switzerland." The festivities include silly hats with feathers, colorful flags, an exotic animal race and a decorated bamboo throne for Mother. The pirates hear the hubbub and attack. The family and Roberta fight back but they're down to the last of their ammunition when Roberta's grandfather's ship sails into view and chases the pirates away. Ernst returns to Europe on the Captain's ship to go to college, and Fritz and Roberta stay on the island to get married and live with Father, Mother and Francis.

RATE THIS ATTRACTION
- Never. Again.
- Not so hot.
- Pretty cool...
- Way cool!
- Awesome!!
- AHH, MY FAVE!!!

One word I'd use to describe this attraction:
_____

FUN FACT
The golden scarab beetle inside your magic carpet is just like the one Jafar uses to make the treasure-filled Cave of Wonders appear in "Aladdin."

MAGICAL!

★ The Magic Carpets of Aladdin

Outdoor Spinning Ride • Lively & exciting • EST. 2001

It's a whole new world from atop a magical flying carpet! Swaying palm trees, golden camels and joyful Middle Eastern music create a **splendid setting** for your high-flying adventure. You'll climb onto a carpet with two rows of pillow-shaped seats and **twirl** around a column topped with Genie's golden lamp. Each of the rows has different controls. If you're up front, you can move a **lever** to make the carpet go up and down. If you're in back, you can press a **golden scarab beetle** to tilt it forward or backward. Hold on tight and enjoy your flight over **Agrabah!**

HOT TIP: **Watch out**—the camels around The Magic Carpets of Aladdin sometimes spit!

SPY: Be sure to check out the ride's central column to see **Abu the Monkey** and **Genie**.

★ Meet n' Greets

Steal a moment with **Aladdin characters** like Jasmine and Aladdin across from The Magic Carpets of Aladdin.

TIME MACHINE

1700s — Aladdin's story is added to "Arabian Nights," a collection of Middle Eastern folktales.

1992 — "Aladdin" hits theaters. Wonderful! Magnificent! Glorious! Punctual!

1992 — The spitting camels debut in Aladdin's Royal Caravan, a parade in Disney's Hollywood Studios.

2001 — The Magic Carpets of Aladdin debuts in Magic Kingdom.

"It's all so magical!"
—JASMINE

The Story of Aladdin

In the city of Agrabah lives a poor, streetsmart young man named Aladdin and his pet monkey Abu. Nearby in the palace, a spirited princess named Jasmine lives with her father the Sultan and her pet tiger Rajah. When Jasmine's father tries to force her to marry a prince, she runs away from the palace and meets Aladdin and Abu who save her from danger in the marketplace. The Sultan's advisor is an evil schemer named Jafar who plots with his talking parrot Iago to take over Agrabah. Jafar lies to Jasmine and tells her Aladdin has been killed when really he has sent Aladdin and Abu to get a golden lamp from a magical underground Cave of Wonders. After Aladdin finds the lamp and a friendly Magic Carpet in the cave, Abu greedily grabs at some forbidden treasure which causes the cave to collapse. Now trapped, Aladdin rubs the lamp to see if there's something written on it and is surprised to see Genie come out of it and offer to grant him three wishes! When Genie tells Aladdin he doesn't like being a slave to the lamp, Aladdin promises he'll use his last wish to set Genie free. Thinking the lamp is lost, Jafar plots to marry Jasmine and control Agrabah that way. Meanwhile Aladdin has Genie transform him into the fabulous Prince Ali so he can impress Jasmine. "Prince Ali" takes Jasmine for a ride around the world on the Magic Carpet and Jasmine realizes he's the same guy she met in the marketplace. Jafar captures Aladdin and tries to drown him but he's saved by Genie, thereby using up his second wish. Iago and Jafar steal the lamp and Jafar becomes Genie's new master. When Jafar makes Genie turn him into the world's most powerful sorcerer, Aladdin tricks Jafar into wishing to be a genie and traps him in a lamp. Aladdin uses his last wish to set Genie free and the Sultan changes Agrabah's laws so Jasmine can marry anyone she wants—like Aladdin!

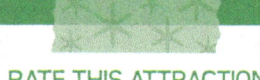

RATE THIS ATTRACTION
- ☐ Never. Again.
- ☐ Not so hot.
- ☐ Pretty cool...
- ☐ Way cool!
- ☐ Awesome!!
- ☐ AHH, MY FAVE!!!

One word I'd use to describe this attraction:
_____

FUN FACT
Enchanted Tiki Room was one of the first attractions EVER to use Audio-Animatronics.

REALLY?!

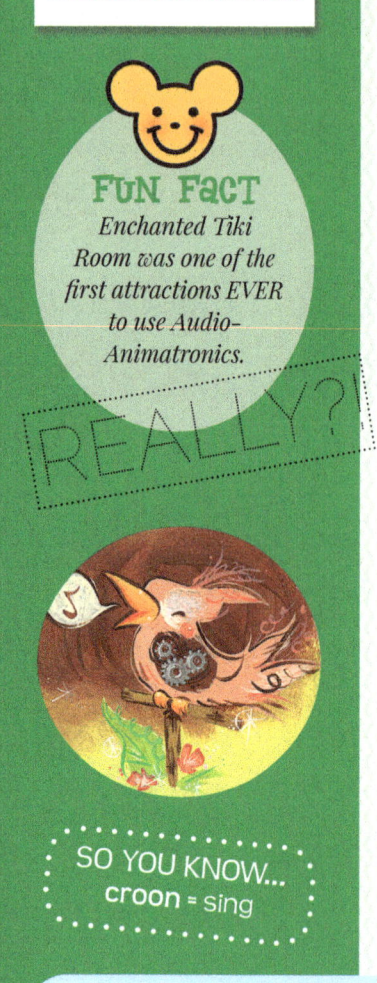

SO YOU KNOW...
croon = sing

Enchanted Tiki Room

INDOOR SHOW — est. 1971 — Lively & exciting

The birds sing words and the flowers **croon** in the Tiki Room! You can't miss the incredible grass-roofed *ceremonial house* that's home to this true classic. Before the show begins, gather near the entrance to enjoy the playful *antics* of two talking toucans. As jungle drums play, you'll head indoors and find a seat to be whisked away to the South Seas on a *musical* journey. Around you, over *200* colorful birds, totem poles, tiki sculptures and tropical flowers fill the room. Comical parrots José, Michael, Pierre and Fritz are your hosts as the *enchanted* room comes alive with songs, a dazzling fountain and even an electrifying storm!

HOT TIP: See if you know **the song** that plays as you're exiting Enchanted Tiki Room. You can hear the same tune while on **Seven Dwarfs Mine Train!**

Illustration by Lisa Penney • www.lisapenney.com

TIME MACHINE

1933
Aloha! Tiki culture begins when the first Don the Beachcomber restaurant opens in Hollywood.

1971
Tropical Serenade is an Opening Day attraction in Magic Kingdom & is renamed The Enchanted Tiki Room in 1996.

1998
The Enchanted Tiki Room Under New Management debuts featuring Iago from "Aladdin" & Zazu from "The Lion King."

2011
The attraction returns to its original format & reopens as Walt Disney's Enchanted Tiki Room.

"But we hope you will always remember the amazing things which happened here, in Walt Disney's Enchanted Tiki Room!"
—PIERRE

RATE THIS ATTRACTION
- ■ Never. Again.
- ■ Not so hot.
- ■ Pretty cool...
- ■ Way cool!
- ■ Awesome!!
- ■ AHH, MY FAVE!!!

One word I'd use to describe this attraction:
_____

★ Jungle Cruise

Outdoor Boat Ride • Lively & Exciting • EST. 1971

It's a jungle out there! But fear not—a daring skipper from the **Jungle Navigation Co.** will guide you safely through the murky waters with an endless supply of **knee-slapping** jokes. To begin your globe-trotting journey, you'll wind past trunks, crates and other expedition supplies to catch a **tramp steamer** boat. Once aboard, you'll **explore** South America's Amazon rainforest, Africa's Congo and Nile rivers, and Asia's Mekong river. You'll **cruise** by amusing animals, a thundering waterfall, the dark ruins of an ancient temple and more before **heading** past salesman Trader Sam on your way back to civilization!

HOT TIP — The fun starts before you even board your Jungle Cruise boat. Listen up for **funny announcements** while you wait to board.

FUN FACT
The Jungle Cruise skippers' outfits have the letters "JNC" on them which stands for Jungle Navigation Co.

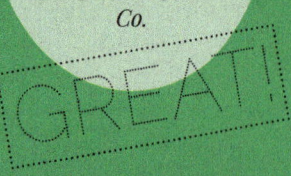

GREAT!

EXCURSION LEDGER
Each Jungle Cruise boat is named after a real river. What was the boat you rode on called?
_____

TOURS DEPARTING DAILY

TIME MACHINE

1951 — "The African Queen" hits theaters & later becomes a major influence on the design of Jungle Cruise.

1971 — Jungle Cruise is an Opening Day attraction in Magic Kingdom.

2013 — An annual tradition begins when Jungle Cruise becomes Jingle Cruise during the holiday season.

2015 — Kungaloosh! The Jungle Navigation Co. Ltd. Skipper Canteen restaurant opens.

animal Hunt!

Put a ✓ in the box next to the **animals** you can see on **Jungle Cruise.** *Answers on page 191.*

143

RATE THIS ATTRACTION
- ☐ Never. Again.
- ☐ Not so hot.
- ☐ Pretty cool...
- ☐ Way cool!
- ☐ Awesome!!
- ☐ AHH, MY FAVE!!!

One word I'd use to describe this attraction:

_____

FUN FACT
The beautiful Castillo del Morro Fortress that is home to Pirates of the Caribbean is inspired by a 16th-century fortress called Castillo San Felipe del Morro in Puerto Rico, a U.S. territory south of Florida.

BUENO!

★ Pirates of the Caribbean

INDOOR Boat Ride · est. 1973 · Lively & exciting

MAY BE SCARY

If ye be brave, or fool enough, proceed! Pass by the tall clocktower to enter *Castillo del Morro Fortress* and travel back to the Golden Age of Piracy. You'll board a barge and sail past the *skeletal remains* of unlucky pirates as the wind roars and an eerie voice chants, "Dead men tell no tales..." After you *plummet* down a waterfall in the darkness, you'll round a bend to witness a fierce *battle* between Captain Barbossa's *galleon* and a Caribbean fort. Heading into port, the town is abuzz with a lively *auction* and talk of the whereabouts of Captain Jack Sparrow and some missing *treasure.* As the town burns around them, the pirates sing about their way of life while Sparrow sits back and enjoys his loot.

SPY — There are many **human** skeletons inside Pirates of the Caribbean but see if you can spot any **mermaid** skeletons.

★ That's Entertainment

The Captain shares his best tips at *Captain Jack Sparrow's Pirate Tutorial* at an outdoor stage across from Pirates of the Caribbean.

TIME MACHINE

1973 — Pirates of the Caribbean opens in Magic Kingdom.

2003 — "Pirates of the Caribbean" hits theaters.

2006 — Avast, mateys! Characters from the popular "Pirates of the Caribbean" movie series are added to the ride.

2013 — A Pirate's Adventure ~ Treasures of the Seven Seas debuts in Magic Kingdom.

"If ye be brave or fool enough to face a pirates' curse, proceed."
—DAVY JONES

a Pirate's Life For you

Step inside **The Crow's Nest** to set sail for **A Pirate's Adventure ~ Treasures of the Seven Seas.** In this free interactive adventure, you'll look for **treasure** and help Captain Jack defeat foes like **Blackbeard the Pirate.** You'll get a special map, a magic talisman and training from a Cast Member on how to unlock cool secrets throughout Adventureland. Finish all five missions to earn a **collectible card** signed by Jack himself.

DID YOU EAT IN ADVENTURELAND?
☐ Yes ☐ No
If yes, where?

_____

What'd ya have?

_____

_____

_____

Was it good?
☐ Yes ☐ No
☐ Maybe So

FUN FACT
You may notice a pirate lass on the sign for Tortuga Tavern. That's Arabella Smith from the Pirates of the Caribbean book series.

SAVVY?

★ Food & Drinks

Aloha Isle

Topped by a tiki-riffic roof, this walk-up stand serves one of Magic Kingdom's most famous treats—the Dole Whip! Tucked right next to Enchanted Tiki Room, you can get your treat to go or enjoy it at a nearby table.
• Dole Whip • Dole Whip float

HOT TIP It's A-OK to take your **Dole Whip**—or any other snack—into Enchanted Tiki Room.

Skipper Canteen

Ready to try some world-famous jungle cuisine? Step inside the headquarters of the Jungle Navigation Co. to dine in the large and airy Mess Hall, the jewel-toned Jungle Room or the cozy S.E.A. Room—which stands for Society of Explorers and Adventurers.
• Baked pasta • Falafel • Fried fish • Noodle bowls • Salads

SPY Check out the **funny book titles** like *Primates of the Caribbean* on the shelves lining the **"secret" passageway** to the S.E.A. Room.

Sunshine Tree Terrace

This two-story baby blue building with breezy fans is home to Orange Bird and his scrumptious orange-and-vanilla Citrus Swirl.
• *Citrus Swirl* • *Citrus Swirl float* • *Ice coffee*

HOT TIP There's **covered seating** between **Sunshine Tree Terrace** and **Zanzibar Trading Co.**

Tortuga Tavern

Bright tropical colors, tile floors and beamed ceilings transport you to the Caribbean island of Tortuga back when dastardly pirates ruled the seas. Enjoy your meal inside the quick-service tavern or find a table on the patio.
• *Cookies* • *Hot dogs* • *Turkey legs*

SPY Look inside for a **barrel** with the words **El Pirata y Perico**—the old name of Tortuga Tavern meaning **The Pirate and the Parakeet** in Spanish.

"Mom, are you sure this water's sanitary? It looks questionable to me."
—TANTOR

Orange You a Cute Little Bird

Nice!

Orange Bird was first spotted in Magic Kingdom in **1971** at Sunshine Tree Terrace. The friendly feathered fellow helped promote Florida orange juice and Walt Disney World in magazine ads, TV commercials, comics, cartoons and a popular book and record set. Orange Bird used to stroll around Magic Kingdom meeting Guests but faded from view in the 1980s. In 2004, **Tokyo Disneyland** re-introduced him as part of their "Orange Day" celebration where he was a **huge hit.** By 2009, Orange Bird souvenirs began reappearing in Walt Disney World again. Today he's well on his way to becoming **more popular** than ever!

SPY See if you can find an **Orange Bird statue** at Sunshine Tree Terrace.

★ ## Sample Souvenirs

"I've waited years for this."
—CAPTAIN HOOK

Pirate Makeover

Dare to get an adventurous pirate or mermaid makeover at **The Pirates League.** Packages include goodies like hats, swords, jewelry, clothing, temporary tattoos and a new name to go with your new look!

HOT TIP Ask **Cast Members** about **personalizing** maps, swords and other souvenirs in the shop next door, **Plaza del Sol Caribe Bazaar.**

Rare Rocks

Explore the cart of unique rocks and crystals at **Agrabah Bazaar** to choose your favorite. Some are so thin you can see through them, some are perfectly round and smooth, and others are dull and bumpy until you turn them over to discover their sparkling interior—diamonds in the rough!

HOT TIP You'll also find rock souvenirs in Frontierland's **Frontier Trading Post** and **other shops** around the resort.

Disney Legend Close-Up: Harriet Burns

Harriet Burns was born in Texas in 1928 and was an imaginative and creative kid who would make her own toys. Her father told her he'd **only** pay for her go to college if she studied **Home Economics** but once she got there she changed her major to **Art.** After getting married and having a daughter, she and her family moved to **Los Angeles** where she worked part-time designing and producing props for TV shows, hotels and Santa's Village theme park. Next, Harriet began working at the **Walt Disney Studios** where she created sets and props for *The Mickey Mouse Club* television show and movies like *Babes In Toyland* and *Mary Poppins*. Later, Harriet became the **very first** female Imagineer ever. Harriet was known for being **best dressed** in skirts, gloves and high heels. Ready for anything, she carried a pair of pants with her to change into in case she had to do rough work. Harriet used her amazing **building** and **painting** skills to help create Enchanted Tiki Room, Haunted Mansion, Pirates of the Caribbean and more. For the **1964 New York World's Fair** she helped design Great Moments with Mr. Lincoln, It's a Small World and Carousel of Progress. Harriet was named a Disney Legend in **2000**.

This Way, That Way, Yonder!

Search up and down **Adventureland** to find these exotic sights. Put a ✓ in the box next to the ones you find.

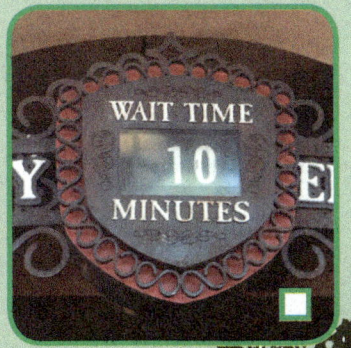

It's always a good idea to look up and notice special details like weather vanes, interesting lights—or carved water buffalos.

Frontierland

What Will You Find in This Chapter?

ATTRACTIONS
- Big Thunder Mountain Railroad
- Country Bear Jamboree
- Splash Mountain
- Tom Sawyer Island
- Walt Disney World Railroad

FOOD & DRINKS
- Golden Oak Outpost
- Pecos Bill Tall Tale Inn and Café
- Westward Ho

MEET N' GREETS
- Country Bears

ACTIVITIES, GAMES & INFO
- Musical Instrument Scrambles!
- Oh, Shoot!
- Canary in a Gold Mine
- What is This Nonsense?
- Where Do I Work?
- Sample Souvenirs
- Disney Legend Close-up: Tony Baxter
- This Way, That Way, Yonder!

MAP OF FRONTIERLAND

KEY
- ATTRACTIONS
- FOOD & DRINKS
- RESTROOMS
- SHOPS

The Rivers of America

RESTROOM

Tom Sawyer Island

Catch rafts to the island here!

RESTROOM

Big Thunder Mountain Railroad

RESTROOM

Walt Disney World Railroad

Splashdown Photos

Splash Mountain

Laughin' Place

Briar Patch

Westward Ho

Big Al's

Pecos Bill Tall Tale Inn and Cafe

Country Bear Jamboree

Frontier Trading Post

Golden Oak Outpost

Prairie Outpost and Supply

LIBERTY SQUARE >

Frontierland Shootin' Arcade

ADVENTURELAND ∨

ADVENTURELAND ∨

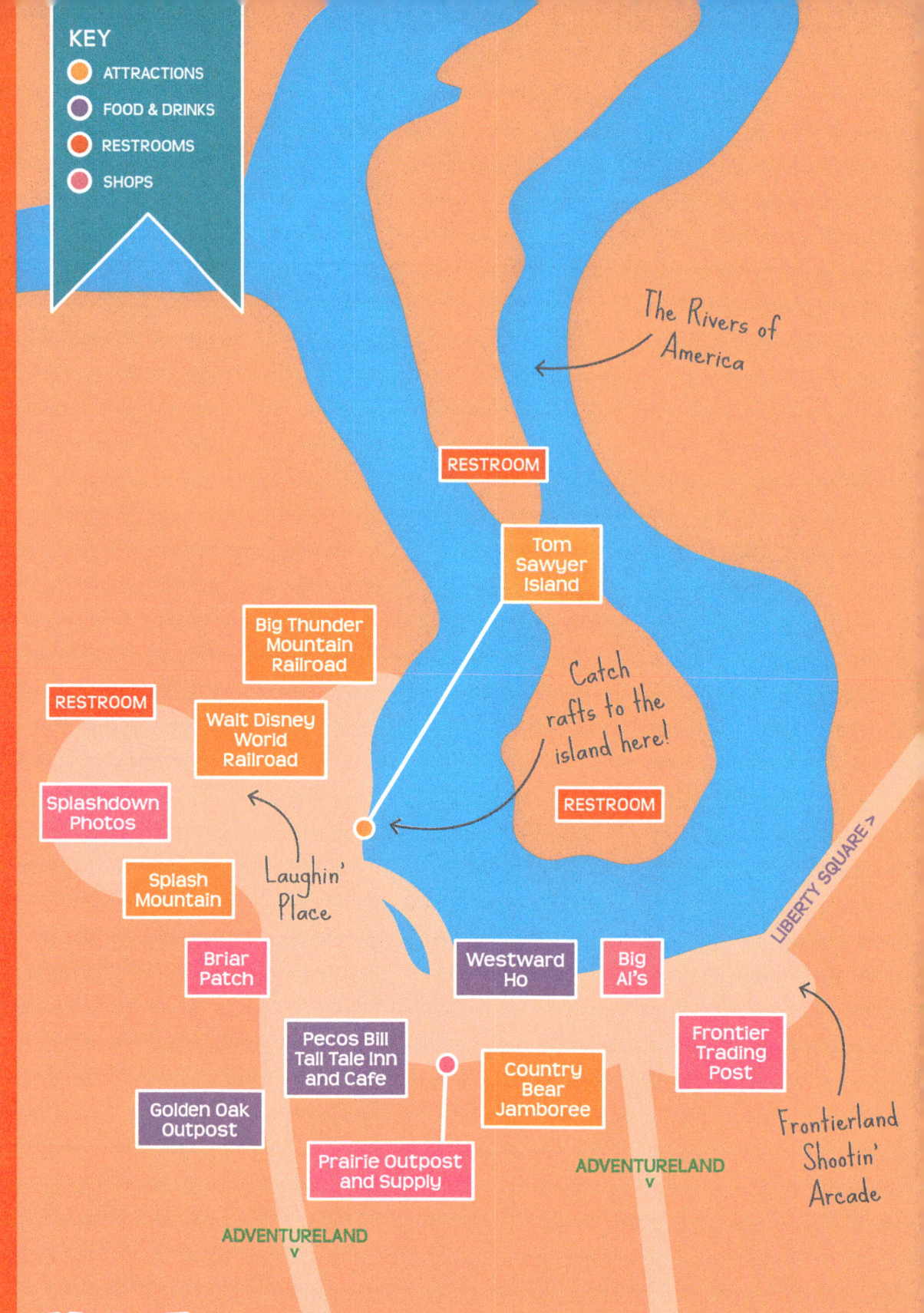

> "I meant to behave but there were too many other options."
> —TOM SAWYER

Pioneer Spirit

Blaze a trail to fun in Frontierland! Back in the 1800s, much of America was wild and unsettled, and **pioneers** were heading west by the thousands to explore the unknown **frontier.** Just like in those **rootin'-tootin'** times, you'll find woodsy log cabins, Western-style **clapboard** buildings and Mexican-style **adobe** structures. Along the walkways, red boulders, rustic log fences and prickly cacti create a mighty fine setting to rustle up some good times!

HOT TIP: Don't miss strolling along the **boardwalk** that runs beside the Rivers of America starting near the **Westward Ho** food stand.

SO YOU KNOW...
pioneers = people who are the first to settle in an area

Waiting Game!

apple   Bacon   CHURRO

ALPHABET RODEO

Players think of a category—like foods in Magic Kingdom—and take turns naming something from that category in alphabetical order. You may have to get creative when you get to letters like "Q" and "Z"! Players continue, taking turns in order until the end of the alphabet is reached.

RATE THIS ATTRACTION
- ☐ Never. Again.
- ☐ Not so hot.
- ☐ Pretty cool…
- ☐ Way cool!
- ☐ Awesome!!
- ☐ AHH, MY FAVE!!!

One word I'd use to describe this attraction:
_____

FUN FACT
The movies "Mission to Mars," "The Country Bears," "Pirates of the Caribbean," & "The Haunted Mansion" were inspired by Disney attractions.

OH!

★ Country Bear Jamboree

INDOOR SHOW — EST. 1971 — CALM & MELLOW

Clap your hands and stomp your feet for the Country Bears! You'll head on into *Grizzly Hall* and take a seat to drink in this musical hoedown starring a cast of funny, furry bears. The show takes place on *five* stages and even mounted *trophy heads* on the wall named Melvin, Max and Buff join in on the fun. Your host Henry will welcome you and introduce the *toe-tapping* acts including the Five Bear Rugs "Zeke and Zeb and Ted and Fred and a bear named Tennessee," the Sun Bonnets and glamorous Teddi Barra who comes down from the ceiling on a *rose-covered* swing. As you exit, Melvin, Max, Buff, Henry and a *racoon* named Sammy sing about how they hope you'll be coming back again!

SPY — Take a sec to check out the **portraits** in the lobby of **Grizzly Hall**. You might see someone you recognize once you head into the show.

Musical Instrument Scrambles!

Unscramble the names of the **instruments** some of the Country Bears play. The first one's been done for you. *Answers on page 191.*

DRAWSOHBA Washboard	URIGAT	DDELIF
ANIOP	JOBNA	MHARNOCAI

TIME MACHINE

1960s — Imagineers work on a bear-themed show for a planned Disney ski resort.

1971 — After plans for the ski resort are scrapped, the show opens in Magic Kingdom as Country Bear Jamboree.

1984 — The Country Bear Christmas Special is the first time a Disney attraction is given a seasonal theme.

1986 — The attraction changes to Country Bear Vacation Hoedown until 1992. Ah, the great outdoors!

Meet the Country Bears

| Gomer | Henry | Ernest | Liver Lips | Wendell |

| Zeke | Zeb | Ted | Fred | Tennessee |

| Trixie | Shaker | Teddi Barra | Big Al | Baby Oscar |

Bunny, Bubbles & Beulah

★ Meet n' Greets

Head across from Grizzly Hall to the banks of the Rivers of America and you may find **Country Bears** like Big Al, Liver Lips, Shaker or Wendell hanging out.

OH, SHOOT!

Not too far from Country Bear Jamboree is **Frontierland Shootin' Arcade**. In this mini replica of Boothill Graveyard in Tombstone, Arizona, you'll find almost **one hundred** targets including cacti, gravestones and a dead tree. Pop your money in the slot, take aim and see how many you can hit. The rifles actually work with **invisible beams of infrared light**. When a target is hit, the object it's on or near will light up, make a sound or move—and **sometimes** it'll do all three!

RATE THIS ATTRACTION
- ☐ Never. Again.
- ☐ Not so hot.
- ☐ Pretty cool...
- ☐ Way cool!
- ☐ Awesome!!
- ☐ AHH, MY FAVE!!!

One word I'd use to describe this attraction:
_____

FUN FACT
Walt Disney was a great admirer of Mark Twain. When the first Tom Sawyer Island was being worked on, Walt didn't like the way the plans were looking so he took them home & designed the island himself.

GOLLY!

★ Tom Sawyer Island

Outdoor play area — est. 1973 — Lively & exciting

Feel footloose and fancy free on Tom Sawyer Island! Relive the **adventures** of Tom and his best pal Huck as you **scramble, ramble** and **amble** around this island in the middle of the Rivers of America. You'll board a **log raft** to travel between the shore and one of the island's landings. Once ashore, you can go whichever direction you like to start **exploring**. Highlights include water flowing uphill in Old Scratch's Mystery Mine, a bottomless pit in Injun Joe's Cave and a wobbly barrel bridge across the water. **Fort Langhorn** is the largest structure on the island and has a blacksmith forge, rifle roosts and **escape tunnels** so you can make a clean getaway if the fort is under attack. When you're ready for a break, relax on a **rocking chair**, play a quiet game of **checkers** and enjoy the scenery. Ahh, this is the life!

SPY — Look for a **bird** who's made a nest in a gear inside **Harper's Mill**—just like in a scene from Disney's 1937 short cartoon *The Old Mill*.

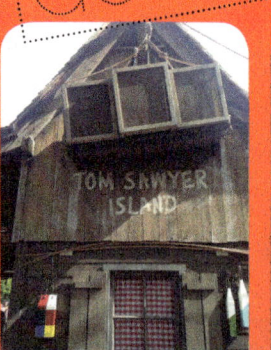

TIME MACHINE

1876 — Samuel Langhorne Clemens writes "The Adventures of Tom Sawyer" under the pen name Mark Twain.

1973 — Two years after Opening Day, Tom Sawyer Island opens to Guests.

1995 — Adventure time! "Tom & Huck" hits theaters.

1996 — Tom Sawyer Island's Fort Sam Clemens is renamed Fort Langhorn.

156

"You can't depend on your eyes when your imagination is out of focus."
—MARK TWAIN

Map of Tom Sawyer Island

- INDIAN TERRITORY
- FORT LANGHORN
- RESTROOM
- POOR OLE JIM'S SHACK
- SMUGGLER'S COVE
- BARREL BRIDGE
- WATERFRONT GAZEBO
- AUNT POLLY'S
- CATFISH COVE
- PAPPY'S FISHING PIER
- SUPERSTITION BRIDGE
- INJUN JOE'S CAVE
- HUCK'S LANDING
- POTTER'S MILL
- OLD SCRATCH'S MYSTERY MINE
- TOM'S LANDING
- RESTROOM
- SCAVENGER'S FORT
- HARPER'S MILL

The Story of Tom Sawyer

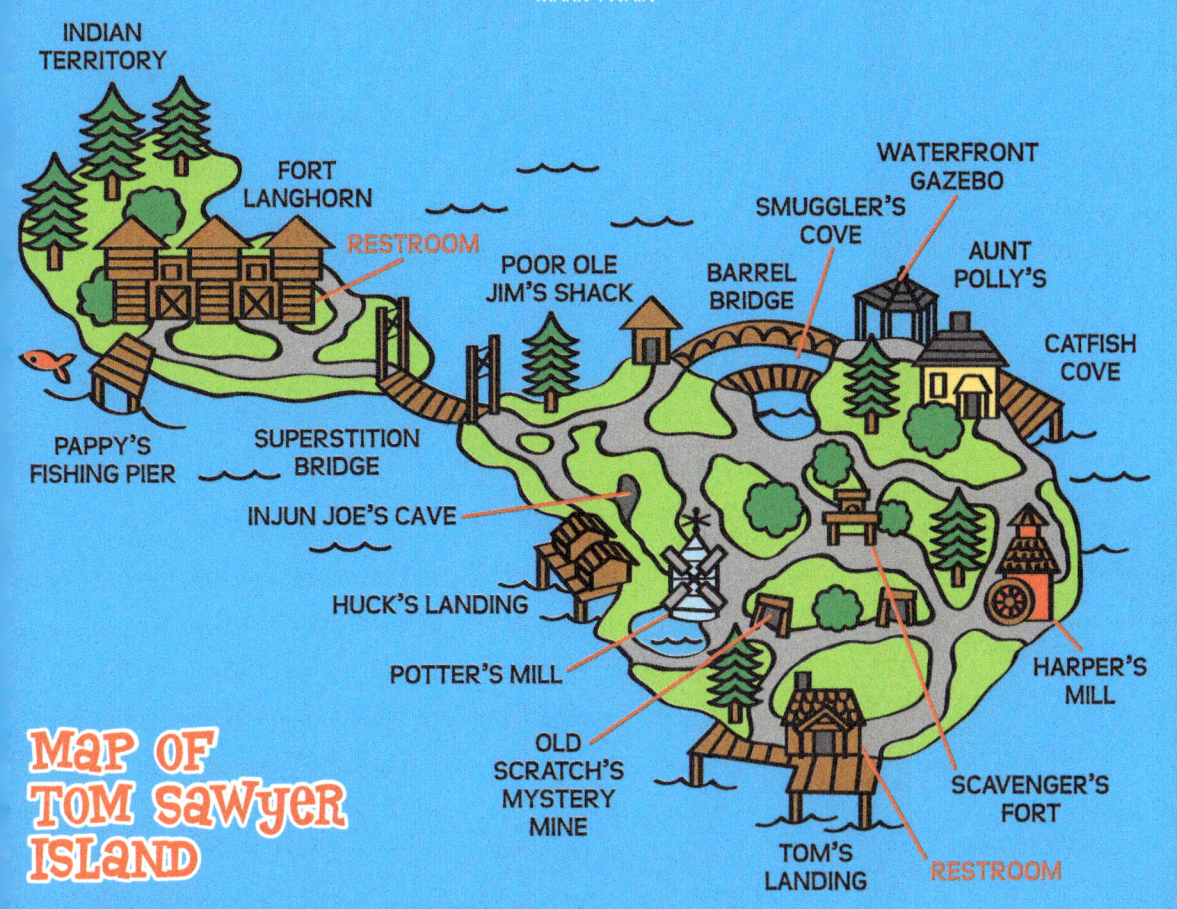

Tom Sawyer is a young boy being raised by his Aunt Polly in a riverfront town in Missouri. Tom falls in love with a new girl in town named Becky Thatcher. After getting into trouble, Tom has to paint a fence as his punishment but ends up tricking his friends into painting it for him. Tom makes friends with Huckleberry "Huck" Finn, a boy who has run away from his father, Pap, and lives on his own. The boys sneak into a graveyard at night and witness a man named Injun Joe killing the town doctor. The boys flee and swear to each other that they'll never tell anyone what they saw. Injun Joe has no idea that anyone saw him and has another man named Muff Potter arrested for the crime. Tom feels guilty that Muff was arrested and he, Huck and a friend named Joe Harper run away to an island to become pirates. After they realize everyone thinks they're dead, Tom, Huck and Joe return and make a surprise appearance at their own funeral. At Muff's trial, Tom steps forward and reveals who the real murderer was, causing Injun Joe to flee. Later, Tom and Huck are exploring a haunted house and spy Injun Joe digging up a buried box of gold. Huck begins to follow Injun Joe for a chance to steal the gold and ends up stopping Injun Joe's plan to attack Widow Douglas. During a school trip, Tom and Becky go in a cave and get lost. While looking for a way out, they run into Injun Joe who's using the cave as a hideout. Judge Thatcher, Becky's father, seals up the cave with Injun Joe inside. Later, Tom and Huck return and find the gold and Widow Douglas adopts Huck and gives him a home. Later, Huck befriends a slave named Jim who works for the sister of Widow Douglas.

★ Big Thunder Mountain Railroad

RATE THIS ATTRACTION
- ☐ Never. Again.
- ☐ Not so hot.
- ☐ Pretty cool...
- ☐ Way cool!
- ☐ Awesome!!
- ☐ AHH, MY FAVE!!!

One word I'd use to describe this attraction:
_____

MAY BE SCARY

This here's the wildest ride in the wilderness! The story goes that *gold* was discovered here back in the *1850s* but members of the Big Thunder Mining Company were frightened away by *ghostly* sounds and scary cave-ins. You'll venture inside an abandoned *mine shaft* to hop on a rusty, rickety mining train. Your journey begins in a dark *cavern* filled with screeching bats and striking rock formations. Once outside, your train *hurtles* through the remains of the town of *Tumbleweed* and its former mining operation. As you dip and dive over hills and through tunnels you'll see spouting water, curious critters and even the bones of a *prehistoric* dinosaur!

Roller Coaster — est. 1980 — Wild & Thrilling

FUN FACT
The towering rocks of Big Thunder Mountain look like the sandstone buttes & towers in Arizona's Monument Valley—a famous symbol of the American Wild West.

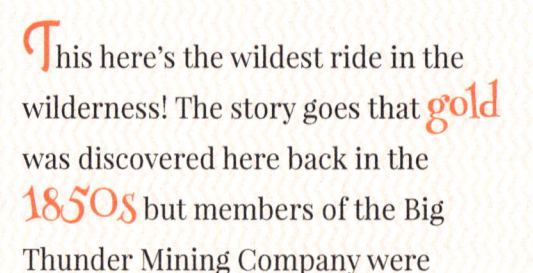

COOL!

SPY — While in line, look for a portrait of the Big Thunder Mining Company's founder **Barnabas T. Bullion** who looks an awful lot like Imagineer **Tony Baxter**.

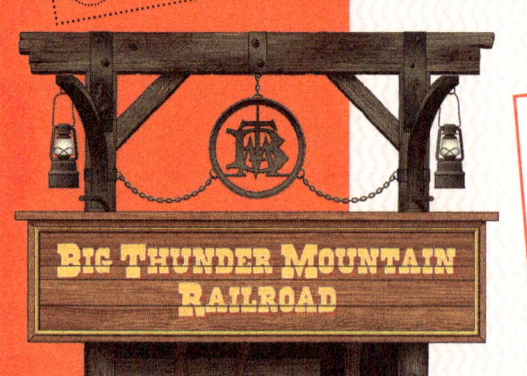

Put a ✓ next to the trains you rode on:
- ☐ I.B. Hearty
- ☐ I.M. Brave
- ☐ I.M. Fearless
- ☐ U.B. Bold
- ☐ U.R. Courageous
- ☐ U.B. Daring

TIME MACHINE

1849 — When gold was discovered in California, the Gold Rush began & thousands of people headed west hoping to strike it rich.

1979 — Disneyland's Big Thunder Mountain Railroad debuts.

1980 — Howdy! Big Thunder Mountain Railroad opens in Magic Kingdom.

2013 — Interactive fun is added to the regular standby line for Big Thunder Mountain Railroad.

Canary in a Gold Mine

Big Thunder Mountain Railroad has funny **AutoCanary** machines to test the air in the mine. Long ago, real **coal miners** would take **canaries** into mines with them. Mining is dangerous work and one of its deadliest hazards is poisonous **carbon monoxide gas**. If there was any of this invisible gas in the air, the little birds would show signs of **distress** long before the workers could tell anything was wrong. This **early warning system** gave people time to escape with their lives. The use of canaries in mines ended in the **1980s** when **carbon monoxide detectors** were invented.

★ Splash Mountain

MAY BE SCARY

RATE THIS ATTRACTION
- ☐ Never. Again.
- ☐ Not so hot.
- ☐ Pretty cool...
- ☐ Way cool!
- ☐ Awesome!!
- ☐ AHH, MY FAVE!!!

One word I'd use to describe this attraction:
_____

LOG FLUME — EST. 1992 — WILD & THRILLING

Stop on by **Chick-A-Pin Hill** to cruise through the tale of Br'er Rabbit! You'll hop in a hollow log and enjoy a mighty pleasant song as you dip down **Slippin' Falls** to visit a colorful bayou. Next, Br'er Rabbit leaves home in search of his laughin' place with scheming **Br'er Bear** and **Br'er Fox** trailing him every step of the way. You'll see buzzing bees, friendly frogs, frolicking turtles, dancing fountains and much more. When the bear and fox **finally** get their paws on Br'er Rabbit, they throw him in the Briar Patch. This is it—the **Big Drop!** Your log will plummet **five stories** at a 45-degree angle to splash into the water below. After winding around the bend, you'll float past singing animals aboard a **grand riverboat** as Br'er Rabbit kicks back at home, safe and sound.

FUN FACT
There actually IS a Laughin' Place in Magic Kingdom—it's a play area right next door to Splash Mountain.

OH JOY!

HOT TIP: You ~~may~~ will get wet.

everything is satisfactual!

WHAT IS THIS NONSENSE?

Draw a line connecting the **silly word** with the **movie** it's first heard in. The first one's been done for you. *Answers on page 191.*

Satisfactual ――――→ Song of the South
Whoop-de-dooper   Cars
Ka-Chow   Mary Poppins
Snarfblatt   The Little Mermaid
Supercalifragilisticexpialidocious   The Tigger Movie

TIME MACHINE

1881 — Br'er Rabbit is featured in "Uncle Remus, His Songs & His Sayings" by Joel Chandler Harris.

1946 — "Song of the South," based on the Uncle Remus stories hits theaters.

1983 — Plans begin for a Zip-a-Dee River Run attraction based on "Song of the South."

1992 — Name change! Splash Mountain opens in Magic Kingdom.

The Story of Song of the South

While a little boy named Johnny is visiting his grandmother's plantation, he makes friends with Uncle Remus, a kind old man who tells folktales about Br'er Rabbit. In one story, Br'er Fox makes a doll out of sticky tar to trick Br'er Rabbit. As Br'er Fox and his partner in crime Br'er Bear watch from the bushes, Br'er Rabbit comes upon the Tar-Baby and says "How do you do?" and is offended when the doll doesn't answer "Fine, how are you?" Thinking the Tar-Baby is rude, Br'er Rabbit socks him in the face, struggles to get loose and gets stuck. Br'er Fox and Br'er Bear come out from their hiding place and Br'er Fox starts building a fire to cook the rabbit for dinner. Br'er Rabbit spies the Briar Patch nearby and has a clever idea. He begs the villains to do *anything* but throw him in the thorny Briar Patch. Br'er Fox does just that and thinks it kills him until Br'er Rabbit reappears and brags about how he was born and bred in the Briar Patch and hops away to safety. Uncle Remus tells another story where Br'er Fox and Br'er Bear try again to roast Br'er Rabbit for dinner. When Br'er Fox goes to throw him in the fire, Br'er Rabbit bursts out laughing and says he's just been to his laughin' place. When they want to see where it is, he leads the villains through the woods and tricks them into walking into a beehive. In the end, Johnny and his friends skip past Uncle Remus singing "Zip-A-Dee-Doo-Dah" when they come upon Br'er Rabbit. Uncle Remus thinks he must be imagining it when the top hat-wearing bluebird of happiness lands on Johnny's shoulder and a bullfrog hops out of the pond after the children. He runs to catch up as a turtle, raccoon, skunk, porcupines and butterflies follow them into the sunset.

Walt Disney World Railroad

Frontierland station is one of the three stops on the Walt Disney World Railroad. *More info on page 54.*

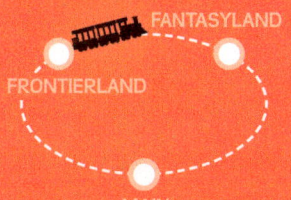

FANTASYLAND
FRONTIERLAND
MAIN STREET USA

SPY — Keep an eye out for some interesting **sights** in between the Frontierland and Fantasyland stations like Native American **teepees** and a family of **deer**.

★ Food & Drinks

"If we ain't got no grub, we sure can't get very far."
—UNCLE REMUS

GOLDEN OAK OUTPOST

Part adobe brick shack, part log cabin, this on-the-go spot is the last outpost for vittels before Frontierland's dead end.
• Chicken nuggets • Cookies • French fries

PECOS BILL TALL TALE INN & CAFÉ

Stone fireplaces, Mexican tile floors and lanterns strung overhead transport you west of the Rio Grande at this quick-service eatery. Turn your meal into something to brag about at the toppings bar.
• Burgers • Burritos • Nachos

SPY: Look around the café to find **Slue-Foot Sue's gloves** and more framed memorabilia from other legends of the West.

WESTWARD HO

The name of this woodsy settler's cabin comes from the 1956 live-action Disney movie *Westward Ho, the Wagons!* Hitch your wagon here for grab n' go snacks.
• Chips • Corn dogs • Frozen lemonade • Soda

DID YOU EAT IN FRONTIERLAND?
☐ Yes   ☐ No
If yes, where?
_____
What'd ya have?
_____
_____
_____
Was it good?
☐ Yes   ☐ No
☐ Maybe So

FUN FACT
There's a pink cabinet in Pecos Bill Tall Tale Inn & Café where Tinker Bell likes to hang out. Ask a Cast Member if you can see if she's around.

OOO!

The Story of Pecos Bill

Pecos Bill was part of Disney's *Melody Time* movie from 1948 which was made up of several short cartoons. As a boy, Bill fell out of a covered wagon and was raised by a family of coyotes. Pecos Bill—named after Pecos, Texas—rescues a horse named Widowmaker and the two become best friends. Bill is a larger-than-life character who rides a cyclone, lassoes a raincloud to make the Gulf of Mexico and digs the Rio Grande river with a stick, all with his trusty horse by his side. When Bill falls in love with Slue-Foot Sue, she wants to get married atop Widowmaker but the animal has other ideas and bucks her all the way up to the moon. Missing Sue, Bill returns to the coyotes and cries every night for his lost love, teaching the coyotes how to howl at the moon just like him.

WHERE DO I WORK?

Cast Members wear **outfits** that match the **theme** of the attraction where they work. Draw a line connecting the **outfit** to the name of the **attraction**. The first one's been done for you. *Answers on page 191.*

Dumbo the Flying Elephant

Haunted Mansion

Splash Mountain

The Magic Carpets of Aladdin

Tomorrowland Speedway

Walt Disney World Railroad

Where would you like to work in Magic Kingdom? Why?

_____
_____
_____

163

★ Sample Souvenirs

"You're my favorite deputy!"
—SHERIFF WOODY

Coonskin Cap

Fur traders in the 18th century wore hats made from skinned racoons. In the 1950s, Disney's *Davy Crockett* TV series made coonskin caps like Davy's all the rage. **Big Al's** carries coonskin caps and other Western provisions to tickle your fancy.

Country Bear Jug

Wet your whistle with a swig from your very own Country Bear jug! You can choose to buy this souvenir container when you order a drink from various food and drink spots in Frontierland.

Sheriff's Badge

There's a new Sheriff in town and their name is —your name! Pick out a personalized badge at **Frontier Trading Post** to let 'em know who's in charge.

HOT TIP: The badges are **pre-printed** so, if you have a **unique name,** you may not find it. There are other **fun choices** though like **Cowboy, Cowgirl** and **Amigo.**

SPY: Look on a sign for Frontier Trading Post to see the name **Texas John Slaughter**—the main character in a **Disney TV show** of the same name.

Disney Legend Close-Up: Tony Baxter

Tony Baxter grew up in Orange County, California and was eight years old when **Disneyland** opened near his home in 1955. Tony grew up building models and was fascinated by the nearby park. After getting to tour the **Imagineering department** as a teen, Tony knew he wanted to become an Imagineer. At seventeen years old, he got a job **serving ice cream** in Disneyland. One day during his lunchbreak, he was trying to sneak a peek at **Pirates of the Caribbean** before it was finished when he ran into legendary Imagineer **Claude Coats.** Claude ended up showing Tony around backstage, neither of them knowing that Claude would later **help train Tony** in the Imagineering department. Tony graduated from college in 1969 where he designed a **Mary Poppins-themed ride** as his senior project. He was hired as an Imagineer and went to Florida to help get **20,000 Leagues Under the Sea: Submarine Voyage** ready for Magic Kingdom's Opening Day. Some of Tony's other **career highlights** include Big Thunder Mountain Railroad, Splash Mountain and Star Tours. Tony was named a Disney Legend in **2013.**

This Way, That Way, Yonder!

Search up and down Frontierland to find these rustic sights.
Put a ✓ in the box next to the ones you find.

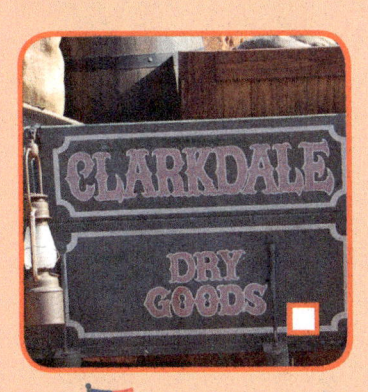

The portals for Sorcerers of the Magic Kingdom also make great photo spots.

The Rest of the World

What Will You Find in This Chapter?

WHAT A WONDERFUL WORLD
An overview of what you'll find in the rest of Walt Disney World

TOP 10 WALT DISNEY WORLD TIPS
Handy ways to get the most out of your visit

GETTING AROUND
The many ways to get around the resort

DISNEY'S ANIMAL KINGDOM
Highlights of attractions, food and drinks, and Meet n' Greets

DISNEY'S HOLLYWOOD STUDIOS
Highlights of attractions, food and drinks, and Meet n' Greets

EPCOT
Highlights of attractions, food and drinks, and Meet n' Greets

WATER PARKS
Attractions you'll find in Blizzard Beach and Typhoon Lagoon

TOP 9 FUN THINGS TO DO IN DISNEY SPRINGS
Fun activities in this popular shopping area

WANNA TRADE?
What pin trading is all about

HOTEL HOPPING
Fun activites at Disney hotels

DISNEY WORLDWIDE
Checklist of every Disney park

KEY
- 🔴 DISNEY HOTELS
- 🟣 SHOPPING AREA
- 🟡 THEME PARK
- 🔵 WATER PARK

Magic Kingdom

GRAND FLORIDIAN

CONTEMPORARY

POLYNESIAN VILLAGE

WILDERNESS LODGE

FORT WILDERNESS HOTEL & CAMPGROUND

Transportation & Ticket Center

Not all bodies of water are shown on this map!

Disney's Boardwalk (entertainment, dining & recreation)

YACHT CLUB

BEACH CLUB

Epcot

BOARDWALK INN

CARIBBEAN BEACH

Disney's Animal Kingdom

CORONADO SPRINGS

Disney's Hollywood Studios

ANIMAL KINGDOM LODGE

Blizzard Beach

ART OF ANIMATION

POP CENTURY

ALL-STAR SPORTS

ALL-STAR MUSIC

ALL-STAR MOVIES

Map of Walt Disney World

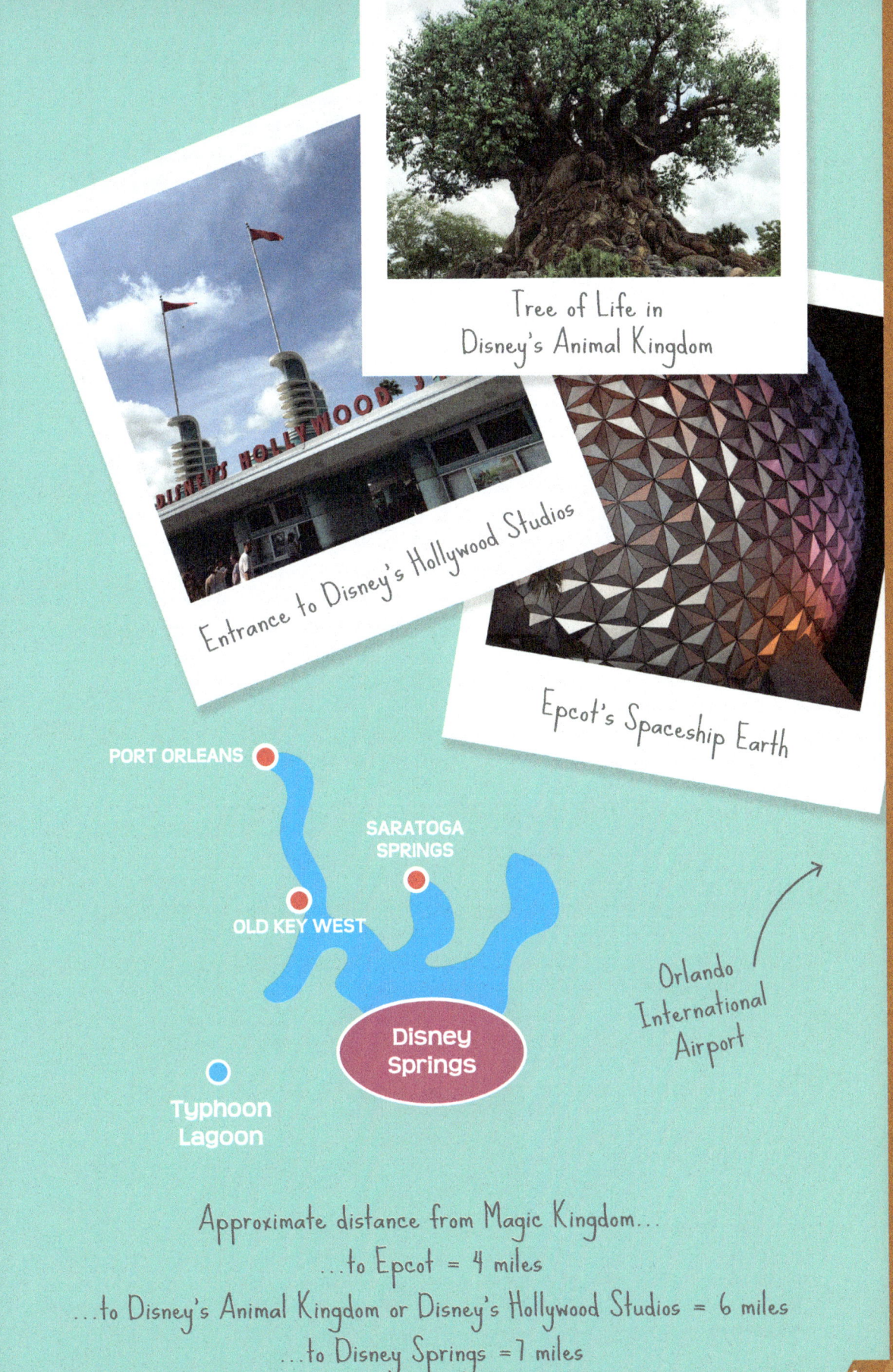

Tree of Life in
Disney's Animal Kingdom

Entrance to Disney's Hollywood Studios

Epcot's Spaceship Earth

PORT ORLEANS

SARATOGA SPRINGS

OLD KEY WEST

Disney Springs

Typhoon Lagoon

Orlando International Airport

Approximate distance from Magic Kingdom...
...to Epcot = 4 miles
...to Disney's Animal Kingdom or Disney's Hollywood Studios = 6 miles
...to Disney Springs = 7 miles

169

What a Wonderful World

Hopefully you'll have time to explore not just Magic Kingdom but all of **Walt Disney World** during your visit. There's just not enough **room** in this book to go into details about **all** of the wonderful things you'll find at the resort but this **overview** will get you started!

HOT TIP: Each day, different parks open early or stay open late for **Extra Magic Hours** for Guests of Disney hotels. The park that has the early opening time tends to be the most **crowded** that day.

Top 10 Walt Disney World Tips

#1 Mornings are **less crowded.** Get to the parks as early as you can!

#2 Have a **good attitude**—if you do, even waiting in line can be fun.

#3 Take time to take **photos**—you'll be glad you did.

#4 Arrange **reservations** for popular attractions, Meet n' Greets and restaurants as soon as you can so you'll have the most choices.

#5 Bring snacks so you don't ever get **overly** hungry.

#6 Rest at your hotel in the **afternoon** so you can return refreshed.

#7 If it's a crowded day in the park, try to eat during **off times.**

#8 If you'll be using it, play around with the **My Disney Experience** app before you go.

#9 If you're staying over several nights, plan a pool day for a break.

#10 Definitely have a gameplan before you go **BUT** be willing to change it.

Time Machine

1971 — Hip hip hooray! Magic Kingdom opens on October 1st.

1982 — EPCOT Center opens on October 1st & is later renamed Epcot.

1989 — Disney-MGM Studios opens on May 1st & is later renamed Disney's Hollywood Studios.

1998 — Disney's Animal Kingdom opens on April 22nd—Earth Day!

Getting Around

Walt Disney World has **free** shuttle buses, boats and monorails to get you where you need to go. For an **extra fee**, you can take express buses, Minnie vans and taxis. For many destinations you can travel **directly** but sometimes you'll need to transfer at the **Transportation and Ticket Center** or another location.

KEY
- 🟠 = To and from Magic Kingdom
- 🟣 = To and from Disney Animal Kingdom
- 🩷 = To and from Disney's Hollywood Studios
- 🟢 = To and from Epcot
- 🔵 = To and from water parks
- 🟤 = To and from Disney Springs

BUS 🟠🟣🩷🟢🔵🟤
You can pretty much get anywhere on a comfy, air-conditioned bus. Buses go from most hotels directly to the theme parks but, to travel to other destinations in the resort, you may have to change buses. For Guests of Disney hotels, there is also a free bus called Mickey's Magical Express that runs between the airport and all Disney hotels.

MONORAIL 🟠🟢
Sleek monorails are powered by clean, electric energy.

HOTELS
- Contemporary 🟠🟢
- Grand Floridian 🟠🟢
- Polynesian Village 🟠🟢

OTHER
- Transportation and Ticket Center 🟠🟢

BOAT 🟠🩷🟢🟤
Ferryboats and cruisers carry you across the waterways.

HOTELS
- Beach Club 🩷🟢
- Boardwalk Inn 🩷🟢
- Contemporary 🟠
- Fort Wilderness 🟠
- Grand Floridian 🟠
- Old Key West 🟤
- Polynesian Village 🟠
- Port Orleans 🟤
- Saratoga Springs 🟤
- Wilderness Lodge 🟠
- Yacht Club 🩷🟢

OTHER
- Transportation and Ticket Center 🟠
- Within Disney's Boardwalk area
- Within Disney Springs

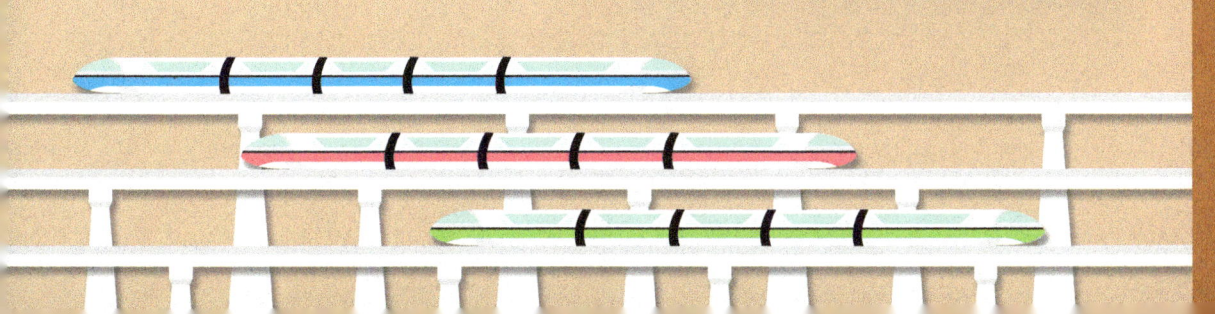

⭐ Disney's Animal Kingdom

*D*iscover the natural wonders of our planet! Wind your way along *Discovery River* as you explore exotic settings in Africa, Asia, DinoLand USA, Discovery Island, Oasis, Rafiki's Planet Watch and the newest land, *Pandora – The World of Avatar*.

HIGHLIGHTS

ATTRACTIONS
- **Affection Section**—Petting zoo with cows, donkeys, goats, pigs and sheep
- **Avatar Flight of Passage**—3D ride atop a winged mountain banshee from *Avatar* through the beautiful world of Pandora
- **Dinosaur**—Thrill ride from the Dino Institute back to prehistoric times to rescue an Iguanadon dinosaur before a meteor strikes
- **Expedition Everest**—High-speed roller coaster through the icy Himalayan mountains—home to a ferocious Yeti
- **It's Tough to be a Bug**—3D movie inside Tree of Life, inspired by *A Bug's Life*
- **Kali River Rapids**—River raft ride through a jungle and Asian temple ruins
- **Kilimanjaro Safaris**—Open-air expedition in a transport truck past over 30 exotic African wildlife species living in the Harambe Wildlife Reserve
- **Na'vi River Journey**—Boat ride through a glowing rainforest in search of a mystical character called the Na'vi Shaman of Songs
- **Primeval Whirl**—Spinning roller coaster-style ride back to dinosaur times

ENTERTAINMENT
- **Festival of the Lion King**—Live, musical celebration of *The Lion King*
- **Finding Nemo — The Musical**—Live, musical retelling of *Finding Nemo*
- **Flights of Wonder**—Exotic bird show featuring hawks, macaws, owls and more
- **Rivers of Light**—Nighttime show celebrating the magic and folklore of nature
- **Tam Tam Drummers of Harambe**—Traditional African drumming and dancing

FOOD & DRINKS
- **Pizzafari**—Animal murals decorate this spot for pizzas and pastas
- **Satu'li Canteen**—Rugged Quonset hut offers a variety of international cuisine
- **Tiffins**—Elegant travel-themed hideaway serving unique gourmet delights
- **Tusker House**—Exotic African setting with character dining
- **Yak & Yeti**—Asian dishes served in quaint building filled with treasures from Nepal

MEET N' GREETS
- Baloo & King Louie • Donald & Daisy Duck • Flik • Goofy & Pluto
- Mickey & Minnie Mouse • Pocahontas • Rafiki • Russell • Tarzan • Timon

⭐ Disney's Hollywood Studios

Hollywood *movie magic* comes alive here! Explore Animation Courtyard, Commissary Lane, Echo Lake, Grand Avenue, Hollywood Boulevard, Pixar Place and Sunset Boulevard. Two new lands—*Star Wars: Galaxy's Edge* and *Toy Story Land*—are opening soon.

HIGHLIGHTS

ATTRACTIONS
- **Muppet Vision 3D**—Movie where Kermit shows Guests around Muppet Studios
- **Rock 'n' Roller Coaster Starring Aerosmith**—High-speed roller coaster with loops and spirals through an adventure with rock band Aerosmith
- **Star Tours — The Adventures Continue**—3D flight simulator that travels to a *Star Wars* galaxy far, far away
- **The Twilight Zone Tower of Terror**—Haunted elevators at the infamous Hollywood Tower Hotel drop into The Twilight Zone
- **Toy Story Midway Mania**—3D shooting gallery ride through Buzz and Woody's world

ENTERTAINMENT
- **Beauty and the Beast — Live on Stage**—Live, musical retelling of *Beauty and the Beast*
- **Fantasmic**—Nighttime show about Mickey Mouse's dreams and nightmares featuring fireworks and special effects
- **For the First Time in Forever: A Frozen Sing-Along Celebration**—Join Anna, Elsa and Kristoff in song as scenes from *Frozen* play on a large screen
- **Indiana Jones Epic Stunt Spectacular**—Live show demonstrating how stunt doubles do their stuff
- **Voyage of The Little Mermaid**—Live, musical retelling of *The Little Mermaid*

FOOD & DRINKS
- **50's Prime Time Café**—Retro 1950's-style diner serving up classic comfort food
- **Hollywood & Vine**—Casual diner with character dining
- **Mama Melrose's Ristorante Italiano**—Cozy setting offering classic Italian delights
- **Sci-Fi Dine-In Theater Restaurant**—Burgers and other American classics served in a retro drive-in movie theater with seating in convertible cars
- **The Hollywood Brown Derby**—Glamorous Old Hollywood-style restaurant featuring gourmet American cuisine

MEET N' GREETS
- Chip 'n Dale • Cruz Ramirez • *Disney Junior* characters • Donald & Daisy Duck
- Goofy • Mickey & Minnie Mouse • Olaf • Pluto • *Star Wars* characters
- *Toy Story* characters

★ Epcot

Epcot is similar to a World's Fair with themes that educate and inspire! There are two areas: *Future World* with most of the park's rides and *World Showcase*, which has a lagoon surrounded by pavilions dedicated to America, Canada, China, France, Germany, Italy, Japan, Mexico, Morocco, Norway and United Kingdom.

HIGHLIGHTS

ATTRACTIONS
- **Frozen Ever After**—Norwegian boat journeys through a Snow Day in Arendelle
- **Gran Fiesta Tour**—Boat ride through the Mexico Pavilion with Donald Duck, José Carioca and Panchito—The Three Caballeros
- **Living with the Land**—Boat tour through greenhouses and laboratories showing where food comes from and might come from in the future
- **Mission: SPACE**—Action-packed thrill ride that simulates a trip to outer space
- **Soarin'**—Hang gliding journey above some of the world's most amazing scenery
- **Spaceship Earth**—A trip inside Epcot's famous silver sphere to explore the history of communication
- **Test Track**—High-tech concept cars are designed by Guests and taken on a simulated test drive of up to 65 MPH

ENTERTAINMENT
- **Films**—The Canadian, Chinese and French Pavilions feature movies about these countries and the American Pavilion has a movie with Audio-Animatronics
- **IllumiNations: Reflections of Earth**—Fireworks show that celebrates humanity
- **Jeweled Dragon Acrobats**—Chinese acrobatic troupe
- **Mariachi Cobre**—Traditional Mexican folk music
- **Matsuriza**—Japanese Taiko drumming
- **Voices of Liberty**—Patriotic American songs sung "a capella" or with no music

FOOD & DRINKS
- **Akershus Royal Banquet Hall**—Storybook castle with character dining
- **Le Cellier Steakhouse**—Canadian château serving gourmet steaks and seafood
- **Restaurant Marrakesh**—Sultan's palace featuring Mediterranean dishes
- **Rose & Crown**—English pub specializing in fish and chips and other British fare
- **Via Napoli Ristorante e Pizzeria**—Southern Italian pastas and wood-fired pizzas

MEET N' GREETS
- Alice • Anna & Elsa • Aurora • Baymax • Belle • Donald Duck • Jasmine • Joy & Sadness • Mary Poppins • Mulan • Pluto • Snow White

⭐ Water Parks

Walt Disney World has two water parks—*Blizzard Beach* and *Typhoon Lagoon!* Each of these parks has its own unique theme. Blizzard Beach looks like a ski resort where the *snow* has melted and Typhoon Lagoon looks like a tropical paradise where everything's been tossed around topsy-turvy by a major storm.

BLIZZARD BEACH HIGHLIGHTS

- **Cross Country Creek**—Lazy river with inner-tubes
- **Downhill Double Dipper**—Side-by-side racing-style tube slides
- **Melt-Away Bay**—One-acre wave pool
- **Runoff Rapids**—Twisting and turning slides with inner-tubes
- **Ski Patrol Training Camp**—Water play area
- **Snow Stormers**—Zigzag slides with mats
- **Summit Plummet**—One of the world's tallest and fastest body slides
- **Teamboat Springs**—One of the world's longest group raft rides
- **Tike's Peak**—Water play area
- **Toboggan Racers**—Racing-style slides with mats

TYPHOON LAGOON HIGHLIGHTS

- **Bay Slides**—Body slides for little ones
- **Castaway Creek**—Lazy river with inner-tubes
- **Crush 'n' Gusher**—Group roller coaster-style raft rides
- **Humunga Kowabunga**—Five-story body slides in the dark
- **Ketchakiddee Creek**—Water play area
- **Mayday Falls**—The park's highest and longest single-rider inner-tube slide
- **Miss Adventure Falls**—Group white-water raft ride
- **Storm Slides**—Twisting and turning body slides
- **Typhoon Lagoon Surf Pool**—North America's largest wave pool

175

★ Top 9 Fun Things to Do in Disney Springs

With shops, a movie theater, restaurants, a hot air balloon, a bowling alley and more, there's plenty of fun to be had in this waterfront shopping area with free admission and free parking.

HOT TIP: Pop into the **Disney Springs Welcome Center** to see when you can catch **live bands and performers,** and **family dance parties!**

#1 Taste Chocolate
Stroll into **Ghirardelli Ice Cream & Chocolate Shop** and they'll give you a free sample of the delicious treat they're famous for. *Sweet!*

#2 Dig for Dinos
Budding archaeologists can excavate dinosaur bones in a sandy pit in the Paleo Zone outside **T-Rex Restaurant.**

#3 Click Bricks
The name Lego comes from the first two letters of "Leg godt" which means "Play well" in Danish. You can play *very* well at **The Lego Store.** You'll find loose pieces to tinker with and racing tracks to test out creations with wheels.

SPY: Look around The Lego Store to marvel at amazing **statues** and **pictures** made entirely out of Lego pieces!

#4 Cool Off
Take a break from the Florida heat and frolic in a refreshing water play area near **Goofy's Candy Company.**

#5 Play with Potatoes
Have fun in **Once Upon a Toy** customizing your own Mr. or Mrs. Potato Head with a variety of cute and colorful accessories.

#6 Window Shop
Can you guess where the World's Largest Disney store is? If you said Disney Springs, you're right! **World of Disney** features twelve rooms filled with clothes, housewares, toys and much, *much* more.

SPY: Check out the mischievous spitting **Stitch** over one of World of Disney's doors!

FUN! FUN! FUN!

#7 Trade Pins

Pin traders shouldn't miss **Disney's Pin Traders,** Walt Disney World's largest pin shop!

#8 Say Cheese

Step in front of a special screen and the talented photographers at **Disney PhotoPass Service Studio** will take your picture and then create a photo where you're in your choice of Disney scenes.

HOT TIP: You can also **preview** and **print out** any PhotoPass pictures you have here.

#9 Ride in an Amphicar

It's not cheap, but a ride in a convertible car that drives from land into the water is truly unique! A friendly Captain will tour up to three passengers around the waterways of Disney Springs from the dock near **The Boathouse Restaurant.** The name amphicar comes from the word **amphibious** which means able to operate on land and water.

Are YOU a Pin Trader?
☐ Yes ☐ No
If yes, what's your favorite pin?
_____

Wanna Trade?

Collectible metal pins can be bought all over Walt Disney World and traded with Cast Members and other Guests. There are **thousands** of pin designs featuring Disney characters, movies, attractions, events and landmarks. Many pin traders put their pins on **lanyards** around their neck but you can stick them on a hat, bag or anywhere you like. If you see a **Cast Member** wearing a pin lanyard, ask them if they'd like to trade pins with you. As long as you're not offering them a pin they already have, they'll probably agree to your trade. You'll also find **pin trading boards** in shops where pins are sold. Keep in mind, if you're asking to trade pins with another **Guest,** it's up to them whether they want to accept a trade or not, just like it's up to **YOU** when you're trading **YOUR** pins.

177

Hotel Hopping

Disney hotels offer many **fun, free activities!** Some of these may require you to be a **Guest** of the hotel, but many do not. When in doubt, give the hotel a **call** and ask. Put a ✓ in the box next to the ones **you** do.

- ★ **CATCH A FLICK UNDER THE STARS**
  Many hotels show Disney movies outdoors on large, blow-up screens.

- ★ **DRAW LIKE A PRO**
  See if you've got what it takes to become a Disney Legend at the Learn to Draw animation class at Art of Animation.

- ★ **ENJOY THE GREAT OUTDOORS**
  Playgrounds, walking paths and nature trails can be found at many hotels.

- ★ **EXPERIENCE THE PAGEANTRY**
  A nightly parade of boats with twinkling lights and music, the Electrical Water Pageant can be seen from the Polynesian Village, Grand Floridian, Wilderness Lodge, Fort Wilderness and Contemporary hotels and outside the entrance to Magic Kingdom.

- ★ **GATHER 'ROUND THE CAMPFIRE**
  Many hotels host campfire stories and songs with marshmallow roasting. Chip 'n Dale appear at the one at Fort Wilderness.

- ★ **GIGGLE AT CARTOONS**
  Many hotel lobbies have a seating area with a TV and kid-sized chairs where they show Disney cartoons and movies.

- ★ **KICK BACK AT THE RANCH**
  Tri-Circle-D Ranch at Fort Wilderness is home to handsome horses, a working blacksmith and a vintage horse-drawn musical instrument called the Dragon Calliope.

- ★ **LEARN TO HULA**
  Sway your hips and learn to dance the hula at Polynesian Village.

- ★ **LISTEN TO LIVE MUSIC**
  The lobby of Grand Floridian is the spot to catch performances by pianists and the Grand Floridian Society Orchestra.

- ★ **LOVE A PARADE**
  Watch the housekeeping team at Grand Floridian carry fancy parasols and parade through the Victorian courtyard around the pool at the start of the day.

- ★ **MARVEL AT MURALS**
  The lobby of the Contemporary features 90-foot-tall tile murals by Disney Legend Mary Blair. See if you can find the five-legged goat!

- ★ **SEARCH THE WILD FOR MICKEY**
  Ask in the lobby at Wilderness Lodge for a guide on where to hunt for the hotel's many Hidden Mickeys.

★ **SEE EXOTIC AFRICAN ANIMALS**
Visit Animal Kingdom Lodge to see the flamingos, giraffes, zebras and other animals that live on the hotel's grounds. Ask in the lobby for a free guide about the animals.

★ **VIEW NATIVE AMERICAN ART**
The lobby of Wilderness Lodge features art, drums, headdresses, painted robes and carved totem poles. Don't miss the totem pole with carvings of Donald Duck, Goofy and Mickey Mouse!

★ **SOCIALIZE WITH BUTTERFLIES**
Spend some time with colorful insects in the Contemporary's Butterfly Garden.

★ **VISIT A MINI RAILROAD MUSEUM**
Wilderness Lodge has a display of Walt Disney's personal railroad memorabilia including art, photos and replicas.

★ **TAKE A MONORAIL**
Hop on and off the Resort Monorail to see the three hotels on its route—the Contemporary, Grand Floridian and Polynesian Village. The monorail actually goes through the Contemporary's lobby!

★ **ZIP AROUND A LAGOON**
Travel from hotel to hotel by boat. Hop off at the dock, explore, and hop back on to see what's next.

Disney Worldwide

If you want to visit EVERY Disney park there is, here's your checklist:

CALIFORNIA
☐ Disneyland Park
☐ Disney California Adventure

FLORIDA
☐ Magic Kingdom
☐ Epcot
☐ Disney's Hollywood Studios
☐ Disney's Animal Kingdom
☐ Disney's Typhoon Lagoon
☐ Disney's Blizzard Beach

TOKYO
☐ Tokyo Disneyland
☐ Tokyo DisneySea

PARIS
☐ Disneyland Park, Paris
☐ Walt Disney Studios

HONG KONG
☐ Hong Kong Disneyland

SHANGHAI
☐ Shanghai Disneyland

If you could go to any of these parks next, which one would you pick?

_____

This cozy seating nook at the Beach Club hotel is full of fun things to spy with your little eye.

HEY KIDS COLOR ME IN!

My Trip Journal

LIBERTY SQUARE

FRONTIERLAND

Main Street USA

ADVENTURELAND

TOMORROWLAND

Fantasyland

My Trip Journal—about My Visit

What was your favorite part of your visit? ....
....

Was it crowded? ☐ Yes ☐ Kinda ☐ No

Which land did you like best in Magic Kingdom?

☐ Adventureland   ☐ Frontierland   ☐ Main Street USA
☐ Fantasyland   ☐ Liberty Square   ☐ Tomorrowland

Why was it your favorite land? ....
....

Draw a picture of yourself in Magic Kingdom:

My Trip Journal—about My Visit

Which theme parks did you visit? If you went to more than one, put a star by the one you liked best!

- ☐ Disney's Animal Kingdom
- ☐ Disney's Hollywood Studios
- ☐ Epcot
- ☐ Magic Kingdom

Did you see any entertainment? If so, what did you see?

....

....

What was the best ride of all? ....

....

What was the most delicious thing you ate or drank? ....

....

Did you see any characters? If so, which ones?

....

....

Did you get any souvenirs? If so, what did you get?

....

....

Was there anything you wanted to do but couldn't? If so, why?

....

....

183

My Trip Journal-Scrapbook

When you're visiting Walt Disney World, hold on to receipts, napkins, maps, stickers, cards, handouts and other flat things to tape or glue onto these pages.

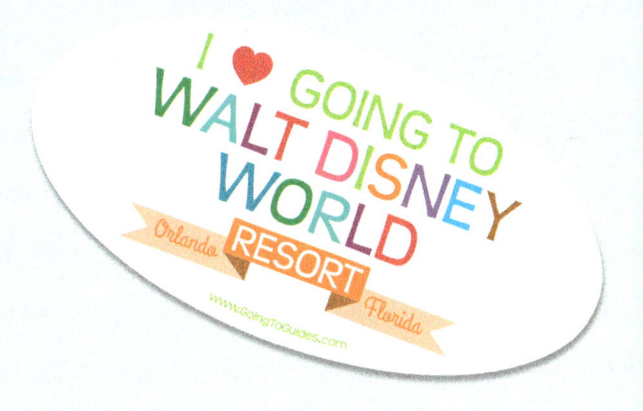

My Trip Journal-Scrapbook

My Trip Journal—Autographs

Characters love to meet their fans and give autographs!
Collect character autographs and stamps here.

My Trip Journal - Autographs

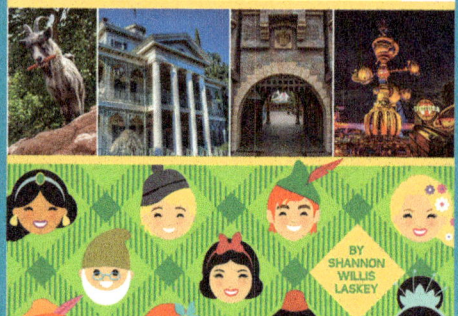

GOING TO DISNEYLAND
A GUIDE FOR KIDS & KIDS AT ♥

BY SHANNON WILLIS LASKEY

GOING TO DISNEY CALIFORNIA ADVENTURE

BY SHANNON

Going To Disneyland & Going To Disney California Adventure
So much more than just guides, these books for kids and kids at heart feature activities, games, quizzes, little-known hot tips & tricks, built-in trip journals & scrapbooks, character autograph pages, info on attractions, food & drinks, things to spy with your little eye, fascinating fun facts & trivia, stories behind the attractions, fill-in-the-blank fun & so much more!

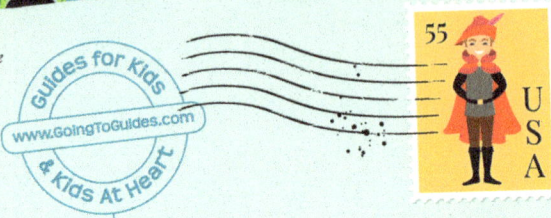

Guides for Kids
www.GoingToGuides.com
& Kids At Heart

Be sure to check out the other Going To Guides for the two parks in the Disneyland Resort in Anaheim, California!

xoxo,
Shannon

To You!

@goingtoguides
www.goingtoguides.com
www.etsy.com/shop/goingtoguides
PO Box 217 • Lafayette, CA 94549

GOING TO GUIDES

Heartfelt Thanks

Oh, where do I begin? So many people helped me to make this book what it is! I'll continue the tradition from my first two Going To Guides and thank my parents first because #1) They are awesome and #2) They are great proofreaders and always see something no one pointed out! Thank you also to my handsome husband and darling sons, Ed and Clark, for supporting me and always giving me great feedback and honest opinions.

Thank you to my friends Toni Morris, Diane Wilkerson Skiff and Cliff Wright who let me join their Walt Disney World gang. Diane (www.facebook.com/MouseFanTravelwithDiane) is also a member of the Going To Magic Kingdom Advisory Board along with EJ Cruz (www.littledolewhips.com) and Julia King (www.instagram.com/mickeymomclub). These three were absolute lifesavers and answered about 5,000 questions from me and were just basically, literally incredible. Thank you to Elizabeth Lewis Cross for taking me on my very first trip to Walt Disney World and always being so supportive. Thanks also to Stacie Smith for accompanying me on my Research Expeditions—you're the best, lady!

Going To Guides are filled with art and photos by myself and other contributors including Going To Guides Official Photographer, Dave DeCaro. I can never thank those artists (listed on the next page) enough for sharing their incredible work with me and I highly, *highly* recommend you check out ALL of their websites.

Speaking of art, we did something new for this guide—a Going To Guides Art Contest! Thank you to judge and Disney Legend Rolly Crump, his lovely wife Marie Tocci and to all who entered and voted. The winning entry by Savanna Rodriguez can be seen on page 76 and the gorgeous entries by the four other finalists are seen on this page. From top to bottom they are by Samantha Daab, Rosa Lopez, Megan Woods and Kristen O'Dell. After the contest was over, I was thrilled to be able to work with all of the finalists to find a spot for their art in the book!

Thank you to Orchard Hill Press for being the best publisher ever and to my genius editor Hugh Allison. This book just wouldn't be the same without him and his incredibly specific questions like, "Does it matter that the term 'grand finale' appears once in the first two books and yet three times in this one?" You'll all be glad to know that I reduced it down to one usage—WHEW! *(EDIT: Hugh points out that by sharing this anecdote, I have now increased it to **two** times.)* Thanks also to Hugh's network of experts including his mum Sylvia Allison, Nick Barbera, VJ Hicks and Sam Berry Cooke—here's another shout-out for your collection!

Last but not least, thank YOU for buying this book! What Going To Guide do you think we should create next? Email your ideas to me at lady@goingtoguides.com. Let's keep in touch! :)

xoxo,
Shannon

Contributor Credits

Throughout this book, all photos and illustrations without a credit are by author Shannon W. Laskey. Illustrations by contributing artists are given a credit on the page on which they appear and are listed below as well. Many images are available for purchase as fine art prints or on other products. Support your favorite artists—and be sure to tell them you saw them here!
All images and photos are the property of their respective owners, but do not imply ownership of what is represented therein.

CONTRIBUTORS:

Aaron Albarran
Snowman, pg. 37
To see more of Aaron's work,
visit www.manandthemouse.com

Dan Bakst
Merida, pg. 92
Mike Wazowski, pg. 99
To see more of Dan's work,
visit www.danbakst.com

Morgane Barret
Robe Cendrillon, pg. 44
Siréne Rose, pg. 85
To see more of Morgane's work, visit www.etsy.com/fr/shop/leroifrankyboutique

Chris Buchholz
Briar Patch, pg. 45
Main Street Vehicles, pg. 56
Ride Vehicles, pg. 57
Main Street Buildings, pg. 63
Gaston's Tavern, pg. 93
Tomorrowland Car, pg. 102
Tomorrowland Scene, pg. 117
Columbia Harbour House, pg. 128
Big Thunder Sign, pg. 158
To see more of Chris' work,
visit www.etsy.com/shop/buchworks

Sam Carter
Extinct Magic Kingdom Attractions, pg. 25
To see more of Sam's work,
visit samcarterart.com

Scott Cocking
Coin Press, pg. 43
To see more of Scott's work,
visit www.sideshowdesign.com

Samantha Daab
Sheriff's Badge, pg. 164
It's a Small World contest entry, pg. 189
To see more of Samantha's work,
visit www.society6.com/scst

Amber Dahl
Monsters, Inc., pg. 112-113
To see more of Amber's work,
visit www.amberdahlart.com

Dave DeCaro
Official Going To Guides Photographer
Vintage Disneyland, pg. 21
Leaky Tikis, pg. 37
The Plaza Restaurant, pg. 60
Castle, pg. 69
It's a Small World, pg. 77
Liberty Belle, pg. 127
Haunted Mansion, pg. 132
Adventureland View, pg. 135
To see more of Dave's work,
visit http://davelandweb.com

Heather Dixon
Haunted Mansion, pg. 125
Mary Poppins, pg. 129
To see more of Heather's work,
visit www.story-monster.com

J. Shari Ewing
Big Thunder, pg. 159
To see more of Shari's work,
visit www.jshariewingart.com

Lindsay Gibson
Halloween Ghosties, pg. 32
Dwarf's Cottage, pg. 80-81
Fruit and Veggies, pg. 95
Burger, Fries and Soda, pg. 114
Pineapple and Dole Whip, pg. 146
The Cheshire Cat, Figaro and Marie, pg. 184
To see more of Lindsay's work,
visit www.etsy.com/shop/emandsprout

Michalina Grzegorz
Tinker Bell, pg. 75
Belle, pg. 83
Jasmine, pg. 139
To see more of Michalina's work, visit www.etsy.com/shop/sketchesofmichelle

danamarie hosler
Hello, pg. 2
Tangled Close-Ups, pg. 47
Alice with Flowers, pg. 90
Fantasyland Scene, pg. 97
Adventureland Scene, pg. 149
To see more of danamarie's work,
visit www.danamariehosler.com

Gabrielle Jean
Prince Charming Carrousel, pg. 70
To see more of Gabrielle's work,
visit www.littlemoondance.storenvy.com

Marisa Lerin
Round date stamps, various pages
To see more of Marisa's work,
visit www.pixelscrapper.com

Rosa C. Lopez
Charm Bracelets, pg. 96
Ear Hats, pg. 96
Cool Ship Sipper, pg. 114
It's a Small World contest entry, pg. 189
To see more of Rosa's work,
visit www.rosaclopez.etsy.com

Kristen O'Dell
Buzz vs. Zurg, pg. 111
It's a Small World contest entry, pg. 189
To see more of Kristen's work,
visit www.instagram.com/kodell728

Lisa Penney
Enchanted Tiki Room, pg. 140-141
To see more of Lisa's work,
visit www.lisapenney.com

Savanna Rodriguez
It's a Small World, pg. 76
To see more of Savanna's work, visit
www.etsy.com/shop/savannarodriguez

Emma Terry
Walt Disney, pg. 18
Pirate Ship, pg. 145
To see more of Emma's work,
visit www.instagram.com/emmat_art

Kirsten Ulve
Tinker Bell, pg. 6
To see more of Kirsten's work,
visit www.kirstenulve.com

Megan Woods
Katrina, pg. 129
Liberty Square Scene, pg. 131
Jungle Animals and Leaves, pg. 143
It's a Small World contest entry, pg. 189
To see more of Megan's work,
visit www.etsy.com/shop/popcutouts

Thank you also to the following amateur photographers who shared their photos: Julia King, pg. 13 and 63; George Miranda, pg. 24; Stacie Smith, pg. 172; Diane Wilkerson Skiff, pg. 175

Game Answers

PAGE 19—Hats Off to Characters!
Left side from top to bottom: Mickey Mouse, Kuzco, Fix-It Felix, Nana, Mary Poppins, Dopey, Moana; *right side from top to bottom:* Jafar, Pinocchio, The Mad Hatter, Prince John, Dr. Facilier, Judy Hopps, Russell

PAGE 47—*Tangled* Character Quiz!
From top to bottom, left to right: Rapunzel, Mother Gothel, Pascal, Maximus, Ulf, Flynn Rider

PAGE 57—A Variety of Vehicles!
Clockwise from top left: Astro Orbiter, The Magic Carpets of Aladdin, Peter Pan's Flight, Buzz Lightyear's Space Ranger Spin, Dumbo the Flying Elephant, Tomorrowland Speedway, Mad Tea Party, Haunted Mansion, The Many Adventures of Winnie the Pooh

PAGE 61—Who Shops Where?
Clockwise from top left: Aladdin, Pocahontas, Judy Hopps, Prince Phillip, Maui, Mulan, Sally, Tarzan, Jessie

PAGE 72—Phony Baloney!
Bibbidi Bobbidi Boogie

PAGE 73—Say What? Attraction Edition!
Clockwise from top left: Astro Orbiter, Country Bear Jamboree, Mickey's PhilharMagic, Big Thunder Mountain Railroad, Peter Pan's Flight, The Magic Carpets of Aladdin, Pirates of the Caribbean, Haunted Mansion

PAGE 89—The Shape of Who?
Clockwise from top left: Goofy, Jiminy Cricket, Timothy Q. Mouse, The Mad Hatter, Marie, Piglet, Lumiere, Sebastian

PAGE 126—Say What? Villains Edition!
Clockwise from top left: Dr. Facilier, Hades, Gaston, Maleficent, Stromboli, Ursula, The Evil Queen, Mother Gothel, Lady Tremaine, Jafar

PAGE 143—Animal Hunt!
Elephant, Giraffe, Hippo, Lion, Monkey, Rhino, Zebra

PAGE 154—Musical Instrument Scrambles!
From top to bottom, left to right: Washboard, Piano, Guitar, Banjo, Fiddle, Harmonica

PAGE 160—What is This Nonsense?
Satisfactual = *Song of the South*, Whoop-de-dooper = *The Tigger Movie*, Ka-Chow = *Cars*, Snarfblatt = *The Little Mermaid*, Supercalifragilisticexpialidocious = *Mary Poppins*

PAGE 163—Where Do I Work?
Clockwise from top right: Dumbo the Flying Elephant, Splash Mountain, Haunted Mansion, The Magic Carpets of Aladdin, Tomorrowland Speedway, Walt Disney World Railroad

Index

- 🟢 = Adventureland
- 🩷 = Fantasyland
- 🟠 = Frontierland
- 🟣 = Liberty Square
- 🔵 = Main Street USA
- 🟠 = Tomorrowland
- 🟤 = The Rest of the World
- 🟣 = Visiting Magic Kingdom
- 🩵 = Walt Disney's World

★ ATTRACTIONS & DESTINATIONS

- 🟠 Astro Orbiter, pg. 106
- 🟠 Big Thunder Mountain Railroad, pg. 158
- 🟠 Buzz Lightyear's Space Ranger Spin, pg. 110
- 🟠 Carousel of Progress, pg. 108
- 🩷 Cinderella Castle, pg. 68
- 🟠 Country Bear Jamboree, pg. 154
- 🩷 Dumbo the Flying Elephant, pg. 86
- 🩷 Enchanted Tales with Belle, pg. 82
- 🟢 Enchanted Tiki Room, pg. 140
- 🟣 Haunted Mansion, pg. 124
- 🩷 It's a Small World, pg. 76
- 🟢 Jungle Cruise, pg. 142
- 🟣 Liberty Square Riverboat, pg. 127
- 🩷 Mad Tea Party, pg. 90
- 🔵 Main Street Vehicles, pg. 56
- 🩷 Mickey's PhilharMagic, pg. 72
- 🟠 Monsters, Inc. Laugh Floor, pg. 112
- 🟠 PeopleMover, pg. 107
- 🩷 Peter Pan's Flight, pg. 74
- 🟢 Pirates of the Caribbean, pg. 144
- 🩷 Prince Charming Regal Carrousel, pg. 70
- 🩷 Seven Dwarfs Mine Train, pg. 80
- 🟠 Space Mountain, pg. 104
- 🟠 Splash Mountain, pg. 160
- 🟢 Swiss Family Treehouse, pg. 136
- 🩷 The Barnstormer, pg. 88
- 🟣 The Hall of Presidents, pg. 122
- 🟢 The Magic Carpets of Aladdin, pg. 138
- 🩷 The Many Adventures of Winnie the Pooh, pg. 78
- 🟠 Tomorrowland Speedway, pg. 102
- 🟠 Tom Sawyer Island, pg. 156
- 🔵 Town Square, pg. 52
- 🩷 Under the Sea ~ Journey of The Little Mermaid, pg. 84
- 🟤 Walt Disney World Railroad, pg. 54
  - 🩷 Fantasyland Station, pg. 87
  - 🟠 Frontierland Station, pg. 161
  - 🔵 Main Street USA Station, pg. 55

★ CHARTS AT A GLANCE

- 🟣 Attractions, pg. 34
- 🟣 Entertainment, pg. 36
- 🟣 Food & Drinks, pg. 38
- 🟣 Meet n' Greets, pg. 41
- 🟣 Shops, pg. 42

★ ENTERTAINMENT

- 🟢 Captain Jack Sparrow's Pirate Tutorial, pg. 144
- 🔵 Casey's Corner Pianist, pg. 53
- 🔵 Citizens of Main Street, pg. 53
- 🟠 Dance Parties, pg. 115
- 🔵 Flag Retreat, pg. 53
- 🔵 Let the Magic Begin, pg. 53
- 🔵 Main Street Philharmonic, pg. 53
- 🔵 Main Street Trolley Show, pg. 53
- 🩷 Mickey's Royal Friendship Faire, pg. 53
- 🔵 The Dapper Dans, pg. 53
- 🟣 The Muppets Present Great Moments in American History, pg. 123
- 🩷 The Royal Majesty Makers, pg. 94

★ FOOD & DRINKS

- 🟢 Aloha Isle, pg. 146
- 🟠 Auntie Gravity's Galactic Goodies, pg. 114
- 🩷 Be Our Guest, pg. 92
- 🔵 Casey's Corner, pg. 58
- 🩷 Cheshire Café, pg. 93
- 🩷 Cinderella's Royal Table, pg. 93
- 🟣 Columbia Harbour House, pg. 128
- 🟠 Cool Ship, pg. 114
- 🟠 Cosmic Ray's Starlight Café, pg. 114
- 🩷 Gaston's Tavern, pg. 93
- 🟠 Golden Oak Outpost, pg. 162
- 🟠 Joffrey's Revive, pg. 115
- 🟣 Liberty Square Market, pg. 128
- 🟣 Liberty Tree Tavern, pg. 129
- 🔵 Main Street Bakery, pg. 58
- 🟠 Pecos Bill Tall Tale Inn and Café, pg. 162
- 🩷 Pinocchio Village Haus, pg. 94
- 🔵 Plaza Ice Cream Parlor, pg. 59
- 🩷 Prince Eric's Village Market, pg. 95
- 🟢 Skipper Canteen, pg. 146
- 🟣 Sleepy Hollow, pg. 129
- 🩷 Storybook Treats, pg. 95
- 🟠 Sunshine Tree Terrace, pg. 147
- 🔵 The Crystal Palace, pg. 59
- 🟣 The Diamond Horseshoe, pg. 129
- 🩷 The Friar's Nook, pg. 95
- 🟠 The Lunching Pad, pg. 115
- 🔵 The Plaza Restaurant, pg. 60
- 🟠 Tomorrowland Terrace, pg. 115
- 🔵 Tony's Town Square Restaurant, pg. 60
- 🟢 Tortuga Tavern, pg. 147
- 🟠 Westward Ho, pg. 162

★ GAMES & ACTIVITIES

- 🟢 Animal Hunt, pg. 143
- 🔵 A Variety of Vehicles, pg. 57
- 🟠 Be An Imagineer, pg. 105
- 🟠 Create a Knock Knock Joke, pg. 113
- 🩵 Hats Off to Characters, pg. 19
- 🟠 Make Your Own Cartoon, pg. 103
- 🟠 Musical Instrument Scrambles, pg. 154
- 🩷 Oh, Pooh, pg. 79
- 🩷 Phony Baloney, pg. 72
- 🩷 Say What, pg. 73, 126
- 🩷 Spin n' Point, pg. 91
- 🟣 *Tangled* Character Quiz, pg. 47
- 🔵 The Pixie Dust Game, pg. 194
- 🩷 The Shape of Who, pg. 89
- 🔵 This Way, That Way, Yonder, pg. 63, 97, 117, 131, 149, 165
- 🟣 Waiting Games, pg. 51, 67, 101, 121, 135, 153
- 🟠 What is This Nonsense, pg. 160
- 🟠 Where Do I Work, pg. 163
- 🔵 Who Shops Where, pg. 61

★ INTERESTING INFO
- A Pirate's Adventure ~ Treasures of the Seven Seas, pg. 145
- AutoCanary Machines, pg. 159
- Closed Attractions, pg. 25
- Disney History, pg. 18
- Disney Parks Worldwide, pg. 179
- Disney's Animal Kingdom, pg. 172
- Disney's Hollywood Studios, pg. 173
- Epcot, pg. 174
- FastPass+, pg. 33
- Fireworks, pg. 36
- Frontierland Shootin' Arcade, pg. 155
- Hidden Mickeys, pg. 40
- Hotel Activities, pg. 178
- Imagineers at Play, pgs. 53, 105, 115
- Interactive Lines, pg. 35
- MagicBands, pg. 33
- Magic Kingdom's Lands, pg. 30
- Main Street Window Honors, pg. 59
- My Disney Experience App, pg. 32
- New York World's Fair, pg. 21
- Orange Bird, pg. 147
- Parades, pg. 36
- PhotoPass, pg. 43
- Pin Trading, pg. 177
- Power Outlets, pg. 46
- Pressed Coins, pg. 43
- Prince Primer, pg. 71
- Racing Flags, pg. 102
- Seasonal Events, pg. 32
- Sorcerers of the Magic Kingdom, pg. 52
- Souvenirs, pgs. 62, 96, 116, 130, 148, 164
- The Muppets Primer, pg. 123
- Top 4 Places to Beat the Heat, pg. 37
- Top 4 Rest Spots, pg. 46
- Top 5 Yummy Snacks, pg. 39
- Top 6 Shops, pg. 44
- Top 9 Fun Things to Do in Disney Springs, pg. 176
- Top 10 Walt Disney World Tips, pg. 170
- Transportation, pg. 171
- Utilidors, pg. 23
- Water parks, pg. 175
- West Coast vs. East Coast, pg. 20

★ INTERESTING PEOPLE
- Tony Baxter, pg. 164
- Harriet Burns, pg. 148
- Roy Disney, pg. 22
- Walt Disney, pg. 18
- Blaine Gibson, pg. 57
- John Hench, pg. 116
- Dorothea Redmond, pg. 96
- Wathel Rogers, pg. 123

★ LANDS
- Adventureland, pg. 133
- Fantasyland, pg. 65
- Frontierland, pg. 151
- Liberty Square, pg. 119
- Main Street USA, pg. 49
- Tomorrowland, pg. 99

★ MAPS
- Adventureland, pg. 134
- Fantasyland, pg. 66
- Frontierland, pg. 152
- Liberty Square, pg. 120
- Magic Kingdom, pg. 28
- Main Street USA, pg. 50
- Tomorrowland, pg. 100
- Tom Sawyer Island, pg. 157
- Utilidors, pg. 23
- Walt Disney World, pg. 168

★ MEET N' GREETS
- Aladdin Characters, pg. 138
- Alice in Wonderland Characters, pg. 90
- Ariel, pg. 84
- Buzz Lightyear, pg. 110
- Cinderella, pg. 95
- Cinderella Characters, pg. 95
- Classic Characters, pg. 52
- Country Bears, pg. 155
- Daisy Duck, pg. 88
- Donald Duck, pg. 88
- Elena of Avalor, pg. 95
- Gaston, pg. 93
- Goofy, pg. 88
- Mary Poppins Characters, pg. 129
- Merida, pg. 92
- Mickey Mouse, pg. 52
- Minnie Mouse, pg. 88
- Peter Pan, pg. 74
- Rapunzel, pg. 95
- Stitch, pg. 115
- Tiana, pg. 95
- Tinker Bell, pg. 52
- Winnie the Pooh Characters, pg. 78

★ THE STORY OF...
- Aladdin, pg. 139
- Alice in Wonderland, pg. 91
- Beauty and the Beast, pg. 83
- Casey at the Bat, pg. 58
- Cinderella, pg. 69
- Dumbo, pg. 87
- Lady and the Tramp, pg. 60
- Monsters, Inc., pg. 113
- Pecos Bill, pg. 162
- Peter Pan, pg. 75
- Pinocchio, pg. 94
- Snow White, pg. 81
- Song of the South, pg. 161
- Swiss Family Robinson, pg. 137
- Tangled, pg. 47
- The Little Mermaid, pg. 85
- Tom Sawyer, pg. 157
- Toy Story 2, pg. 111
- Winnie the Pooh, pg. 79

The Pixie Dust Game

HOW TO PLAY

Tinker Bell is sprinkling **pixie dust** over the citizens of Never Land. Help her by taking turns tossing **game pieces** onto the board. For the game pieces, use something flat like a **coin** or a **pebble**. If your game piece does not land within a point area, you score **no points** for that turn. The first player to score **100+ points** wins. If you feel like you **"never land"** on the right spot, keep trying. All it takes is faith and trust and a little bit of—**practice!**

LOSE 2 POINTS

1 POINT

10 POINTS

25 POINTS

50 POINTS

1 POINT

10 POINTS

LOSE 5 POINTS

"Never say goodbye, because saying goodbye means going away and going away means forgetting."
—J.M. BARRIE, *PETER PAN*

CPSIA information can be obtained
at www.ICGtesting.com
Printed in the USA
BVOW05*0944051217
501911BV00025B/980/P